**Temple Israel Library**

**Minneapolis, Minn.**

———

Please sign your full name on the above card.

Return books promptly to the Library or Temple Office.

Fines will be charged for overdue books or for damage or loss of same.

*The*
*Twisted*
*Wire*

# RICHARD FALKIRK

# The
# Twisted
# Wire

DOUBLEDAY & COMPANY, INC.
GARDEN CITY, NEW YORK   1971

F
F18

All of the characters in this book
are fictitious, and any resemblance
to actual persons, living or dead,
is purely coincidental.

76-51     8-12-71    Feltman  595/480

Part of a quote from a spokesman of the American Embassy in London, following a report in February 1969, alleging that, because of a crossed wire, someone overheard a telephone conversation between the Ambassador and the President of the United States: "Anything is possible with telephones . . ."

*The*
*Twisted*
*Wire*

Three men listened to the President of the United States talking on the top security telephone wire from Washington to London.

Robert Lindsay Bartlett, the American Ambassador in London, for whom the call was intended. He took it in his office in Grosvenor Square and understood every word the President said because they had discussed the crisis the previous day.

Nicolai Malenkov, head of communications at the Russian Embassy in Kensington, still smug from the congratulations from Moscow for succeeding in tapping the Washington-London line. He reported the President's remarks to his superiors in the KGB who partially understood them.

Tom Bartlett, geologist, who was totally confused by the President's observations because he had been expecting to hear the voice of his wife, Helen Bartlett, who worked in the American Embassy library.

Bartlett subsequently decided that the reasons for the crossed wire were twofold. One, he was trying to call his wife at the Embassy. Two, he had the same surname as the Ambassador. But, on further consideration of the British telephonic system, he decided that the wire could have become crossed just as easily without any coincidences of name and timing.

At the time of the call he did not speculate on the reasons for the interception. The male voice on the phone, young, respectful, and possibly sycophantic, said: "This is the White

1

House, Mr Ambassador Bartlett, I have the President for you."

Tom Bartlett put down the ammonite which he used as a paperweight on his desk, stared at the receiver for a moment, then put it back to his ear.

He recognised the President's voice at once. Authoritative, sincere but somehow always electioneering. The President was saying: "So you haven't been able to get hold of this guy?"

The Ambassador said: "You didn't give us much time, Mr President." It was the voice of big business unaccustomed to diplomatic subservience.

"I'm aware of how much time I gave you. We'll have to get to work on it at the other end. Even on the plane maybe."

At this point Tom Bartlett, who suffered from hay fever, was overcome by the pollen count rising in the study because he had forgotten to shut the French window facing the honeyed garden of the country house in Sussex. He sneezed many times and when he picked up the receiver again the President was just finishing with the Ambassador. American prestige, said the President in his whistle-stop voice, was at stake. The Ambassador did not heckle him, but his silence was resentful.

There was a small click mocking the crash with which Bartlett imagined the President cracked down the phone. Then a louder click which sounded as if it emanated from the local exchange. Bartlett rubbed his itching eyes and pondered on the conversation he had overheard. It seemed vaguely as if, at one stage, they had been talking about the Ambassador in the third person. But that was ridiculous: it was his hay fever capsules affecting him again: they stunned his senses, convinced colleagues that he was on hard drugs and had no effect whatsoever on his early summer allergy.

Outside he heard rubber on gravel announce the arrival of the hire car to take him to London Airport. An old Bentley with sighing leather seats and inherited decorum; much more his style, Bartlett decided ruefully, than the serpent-faced jets screaming for their passengers on the tarmac.

The driver who was ageing decorously with the car said: "Where to this time, Mr Bartlett?"

"Israel," Bartlett said. "The Promised Land."

"Ah," said the driver who had taken many passengers to the launching pad but never been launched himself. "More trouble there today. Just heard it on the news. The Israelites made another raid into Egypt." He reproached an E-type Jaguar overtaking him on a bend with a genteel note from his hooter. "I shouldn't have thought it was a place for a gentleman like yourself to be going."

"Is there any reason why I shouldn't be going to a place where there's a bit of action?"

"No, sir. I didn't mean it like that."

But Bartlett knew he did. He glanced at the trousers of his new lightweight suit already bagging at the knees, at the stain from a ball-point pen on his lapel; he peered in the driving mirror and saw the wing of his shirt collar sticking out like a sleeping butterfly, his untidy, finger-combed hair. Indisputably the composite picture was not that of a man of action.

The driver said: "I meant you being a geologist, sir. You can't somehow associate fossils with bombs and rockets."

"I'm going to address the International Geological Society in Jerusalem," Bartlett said.

"Ah." The driver nodded as if the word society explained the incongruity.

The car left the green cushions of the South Downs where as a boy Bartlett had first examined the earth's crust. In a village miming siesta in the May sunshine Bartlett noticed a girl in a miniskirt jogging prettily along the only street, breasts bouncing. He was reassured at his own interest. He poked back the wing of his collar and settled into the protesting cushions.

He was excited about going to Israel. To see the headlines jerk into life like marionettes. To revisit the Negev and the Sinai. To see Jerusalem, Nazareth, Bethlehem, Caesarea.

It wasn't until he was at the airport waiting to be called

3

for the El Al jet that he realised that he hadn't phoned his wife. He glanced at his watch. She would be on her way back to their town apartment in Marylebone High Street by now. He could always explain that he had been delayed by the President of the United States . . . at that moment they called the Amsterdam-Tel Aviv flight.

Chapter 1

The official gunman sat in the front row of the tourist seats. Inside his suede jacket which he had bought in London he carried a Beretta. Just inside the flight deck was an Uzi submachine gun.

Ya'acov Krivine, who was twenty-two years old with bandit good looks, officially hoped that there would be no trouble when the Boeing landed at Amsterdam. Unofficially he envied the guard who had shot the Arab terrorists in Switzerland and hoped that a similar attempt would be made in Holland.

He glanced round at the rest of the passengers. All had been checked. All were clean with the possible exception of the young Polish Jew sitting beside the button-down-collar American diplomat. That, he had been told, was the trouble with Jews who were allowed out of Russia and its satellites: you couldn't always be sure whether the young ones really considered themselves to be Jews or Communists. But Ya'acov was sure that all of them would be Jews once they had lived in Israel.

Behind the Pole and the American sat the Englishman Bartlett whose movements he had been told to keep under observation. He didn't know why. Geologist, fortyish, vaguish. Perhaps he was a British agent; that would explain some of Britain's more spectacular security blunders.

Ya'acov Krivine turned his attention to the Pole and the

American sitting next to him. The Pole was pale and damp and wore unassertive gold-rimmed spectacles and a black suit with broad lapels. The American was just as Ya'acov expected all Americans to be: athletic, crewcut, excessively polite, probably ex-Army and Vietnam. Ya'acov wondered about the scrubbing-brush hairstyles which so many Americans wore and patted self-consciously: he knew from experience that girls preferred longer hair.

The tall, gentle-faced stewardess in the blue uniform just beginning to shine said in Hebrew: "Coffee, sir?" Her voice was sarcastic. This annoyed Ya'acov because he was accustomed to girls who became instantly available on perceiving his looks and wholeheartedly acquiescent on seeing the scar of his Six Day War wound.

"Yes, please." He looked up at her gentle face and recalled that she was a Judo expert as well as a stewardess. "Why are you so hostile to me?"

The stewardess glanced around and leaned towards him. "Because I am tired of tough guys," she said. "Every man in Israel who puts on a uniform thinks he's Steve McQueen."

Ya'acov favoured her with his brigand smile. "I think the Arabs must think so too."

The stewardess who had been attached to the same Army unit as Ya'acov in the Sinai said: "I prefer other qualities in a man."

"You prefer someone like that Englishman who looks like a schoolmaster?"

Ya'acov noticed with surprise and irritation that her expression softened. "Yes," she said. "Someone like that. He's rather sweet." She straightened up.

Ya'acov said: "There's just one thing."

"Really? What's that?"

"Your black belt's showing," Ya'acov said.

He leaned back in his seat, quite pleased with himself, and lit a Savyon cigarette. Below the English Channel was blue and molten. In ten minutes' time they would be landing at Amsterdam. His hand strayed inside his jacket and fingered the barrel of the Beretta. Then he went into the flight deck to check the Israeli-made Uzi. Just in case, he thought hopefully and unofficially.

Five rows behind the official gunman Tom Bartlett obediently fastened his safety belt, extinguished his cigarette and picked up the fawn pamphlet called *Flying Kosher*. The tall stewardess leaned over the girl sitting beside him and checked his belt. She was, he thought, unusually solicitous. He smiled at her and went on reading. "Kosher is knadles, knishes, gefilte fish—all the traditional treats of the Jewish kitchen."

The girl beside him said: "Don't worry too much. It just means you can't have cream in your coffee after lunch."

"I only drink it black," Bartlett said. There was a pause. He smelled her perfume: Chanel No. 5, he decided, because that was the only perfume he knew. He noted her shiny buckled shoes and her neat knees and became aware of the body warmth they shared between them. Again he was reassured by the virility of his observation.

The girl said: "Are you going to Israel on vacation?"

Bartlett half-turned so that he could see her face. Tanned, a little sad, greenish-eyed, finely textured hair worn in a fringe, inquisitive features. Not the sort of face you expected an Israeli girl to have after all those newspaper pictures of women soldiers toting rifles. If, in fact, she was an Israeli. He asked her.

"Yes," she said. "I hope you didn't mind me talking to you. But we are like that in Israel. I know that in the States and Britain it is different."

"I certainly don't mind," Bartlett said. And meant it. "No, I'm not going on vacation—it's a business trip."

"I see." She stuffed a copy of *Maariv* into the seat pocket. "Did you know that we Israeli girls are also very nosey?" She spoke with a slight American accent.

"There's nothing wrong with curiosity," Bartlett said. "It's the foundation of my profession. Which, incidentally, is geology."

7

"That," said the girl, "is quite remarkable, Mr . . ."

"Bartlett," he said. "Tom Bartlett. Why is it so remarkable?"

"Because I too have been studying the soil. Advanced methods of irrigation which have been perfected in the States."

It was, Bartlett thought, quite remarkable. But it had been a remarkable day.

"How long will you be in Israel?" she said.

"About three days in Tel Aviv," he said. "Then two or three days in Jerusalem for the actual conference."

They were interrupted by the voice of the stewardess, first in Hebrew, then in English. "We hope you have enjoyed your flight from London to Amsterdam. We regret that, owing to the short duration of our stay in Amsterdam, passengers in transit will not be allowed to disembark from the aircraft."

"Why on earth not?" Bartlett said. "They'll take at least half an hour to refuel the aircraft."

"You sound like an experienced traveller," the girl said.

"I've flown a bit."

"Perhaps there are other reasons for the precaution."

The aircraft bounced gently on the runway, settled, taxied, stopped. The disembarking passengers departed and with them went the gangsterish young man in the suede jacket.

"Why's he been allowed out?" Bartlett said.

"Perhaps he's disembarking," the girl said.

"But he's Israeli, surely."

"Just because he looks like a Mafia bodyguard doesn't necessarily mean he's an Israeli."

"Look." Bartlett pointed at the tarmac. "He's got into that Volkswagen." The blue Volkswagen began to circle the aircraft.

The girl shrugged.

Bartlett realised then and said: "He's the guard, isn't he? In case the Arabs try anything."

The girl shrugged again. Bartlett watched the tankers refuelling the jet, the patrolling Volkswagen, the officer in El Al uniform scanning the perimeter of the airport with field

.glasses. He shivered, because someone had pulled the strings of the marionette headlines.

The embarking passengers arrived through the hooded gangway that led straight on to the aircraft. Outside the Volkswagen continued to circle like a lost insect. Then the Israeli in the suede jacket climbed out and returned to the aircraft looking rather sulky. The Boeing taxied to the end of the runway, climbed the bright sky and headed towards Tel Aviv, the Hill of the Spring.

Over the Greek islands, pumice stones in the flat water, Raquel Rabinovitz said to Tom Bartlett: "Are you married, Mr Bartlett?"

Bartlett finished the little bottle of red Avdat wine that he had ordered with his meal and smiled. "You would make an excellent geologist, Miss Rabinovitz."

The girl sipped her black coffee. "You are trying to evade the point already."

Bartlett said: "Your curiosity is formidable. Yes, I am married." He lit a cigarette with the gold Dunhill his wife had given him a decade ago and considered his marriage.

"Could you not have brought your wife with you?"

"She didn't want to come," he said. "She had other things to do."

Like drinking and eating and sleeping with a fur-headed Arab from the Jordanian Embassy. And discussing dear old Tom, poor old Tom, with him. No, Israel was decidedly not the country for Helen.

"Is she English?" the girl said.

"No, American."

"And very beautiful?"

"Very."

With a sigh Raquel Rabinovitz changed the subject. "I too come from the States. My parents were Russian but they escaped after the last war because they knew what Communism was all about. They settled in New York. I was born there. Then one day my father said, 'What for should

9

we stay here when we are about to be given our own country?' And my mother said, 'Wherever you go, Doron, then I go with you.' And so we came to Israel just in time for the first war against the Arabs."

There didn't seem any point in asking her questions because all information was supplied unsolicited. He said politely: "So you are not a Sabra, then?"

"Not a true Sabra. But I am one at heart, I promise you."

"I believe you. How old are you?"

"Twenty-three."

"And you served in the Army?"

"Of course—all Israeli girls do."

"What did you do?"

Raquel Rabinovitz looked confused. As confusion seemed out of character Bartlett repeated the question.

"I was a member of the Hiba," she said.

"And what on earth is that?"

"It is the section of the Army that does street police duty. It is very essential work."

Bartlett laughed aloud. "So I'm having lunch with a policewoman?"

"Is that so funny?"

"Not really. Except that it was once my ambition . . ."

"Your ambition to what?"

"Nothing," he said. "Would you care for some more wine?"

"No thank you. You will find that in Israel we have little need for artificial stimulants. Now, if you will excuse me, I think I will sleep a little."

"Of course. I'm sorry if I offended you."

"That's all right, Mr Bartlett. We Israelis do not mind people laughing at us. It's when they start shooting at us that we object." She closed her eyes and Bartlett thought that she looked surprisingly vulnerable for an ex-policewoman.

The islands disappeared and a few parachutes of cloud appeared between the aircraft and the empty sea. Bartlett picked up the green and gold booklet containing 101 words of Hebrew—"the mother tongue of many Israelis whose

10

mothers knew it not." He discovered that El Al meant upward which was reassuring. He put the booklet away with *Flying Kosher* and took his maps out of his old brown-leather briefcase.

Ras Abu Rudeis, Waddi Firan, St Catherine's Monastery. Mountains the colour of rusting iron, morning air that smelled of sharp herbs, waddis green with palms that looked like moss from the granite peaks, wells filled with ice that had never frozen. When he had last visited the Sinai—ten or eleven years ago—it had been in the hands of the Egyptians. Not even the Israelis could have changed it very much.

Bartlett replaced the maps, tucked the briefcase under his seat, and relaxed. Then, after making an abortive effort to keep his mouth closed, he slept.

In front of him the Pole loosened his almost transparent grey tie and snored immediately. The American with the thick cropped hair dozed.

Only the official gunman remained completely alert as the Boeing approached the disputed territories of the Levant. And the pilot and the navigator.

Tom Bartlett was annoyed. "You must admit," he said, "that this is hardly an auspicious introduction to Israeli efficiency."

"It could happen with any airline," Raquel Rabinovitz said. "In fact El Al is one of the most efficient airlines in the world. Did you know that since the two Arab attacks they have carried more passengers than ever before?"

"I didn't know," Bartlett said. "Nor do I quite see what it's got to do with the fact that they've lost my suitcase."

"Perhaps the London Airport porters forgot to load it. Or perhaps the Dutch unloaded it by mistake at Amsterdam."

Bartlett smiled despite his annoyance. "But no Israeli is to blame? Even though I personally handed it over to El Al?" He prodded at the errant wing of his collar. He could feel the sweat gathering beneath his tropical suit. He lit a cigarette. "It's not your fault," he said. "You've done as

11

much as you can. But everything I need for my stay here is in that case."

"I understand," she said. "But it could have happened on any airline."

"All right," he said. "But is there anything more you can do?"

"I'll see." She walked away, lithe and smart and aggressive.

Bartlett watched the other passengers pushing trolleys of luggage towards waiting business associates, Jewish mothers, and predatory taxi drivers. He would have liked to have been in a receptive mood to assimilate the excitement and confidence he had sensed as he walked from the Boeing to the arrival lounge. But they had spoiled his pleasure by losing his suitcase.

He noticed that both the crewcut American and the Pole with the gold-rimmed spectacles were waiting around although they had picked up their baggage.

Raquel Rabinovitz returned smiling triumphantly with a customs official and the missing suitcase. "There," she said. "It was muddled up with the baggage off another flight. It could have happened anywhere in the world."

"Thanks," Bartlett said. "Thanks very much." And with uncharacteristic flippancy he added: "What a way to run an airline."

"I beg your pardon, sir?" said the customs official.

"I'm sorry," Bartlett said. "I was joking. I'm very grateful to you for finding my luggage."

"Perhaps," the customs official said, "you would be good enough to open your suitcase for me."

Bartlett said: "Very well." He found his keys in his trouser pocket and opened the suitcase that was even older than his briefcase. He looked at his shirts and underclothes, his papers and his geologist's tools. "I don't think you need examine them too closely," he said. "Someone already has."

Chapter 2

Bartlett first suspected that he was being followed as, town guide in hand, he walked up Dizengoff Street from Dizengoff Circle where a fountain splashed and teenage soldiers with submachine guns on their shoulders munched peta crammed with meat and tehina and humus and stalked the happy soldier girls.

There was no proof; it was merely a new instinct awakened when he realised that his suitcase had been searched. Twice he spun round to surprise his pursuer. Each time he thought he noticed a furtive movement on the sidewalk. But he couldn't be sure: it might have been the overactivity of this new instinct. And there was so much jostling movement in the street. He walked on past the small expensive shops, bookstalls garlanded with *Time, Newsweek,* and Hebrew scandal magazines liberally bosomed and buttocked, past a dozen sidewalk cafes where tourists drank beer and Israelis sipped mineral waters.

Halfway up the broad thoroughfare Bartlett stopped at the Stern Cafe and ordered a Gold Star beer. It seemed to him in his new state of awareness that there were two oiled movements behind him as he turned into the cafe. But, of course, it was all ludicrous. Why should anyone want to follow a middle-ageing geologist who had flown to Israel to escape briefly from a fossilised routine and a faithless wife

13

to present a paper to a gathering of colleagues who would be transfixed to their seats by the familiarity of his material?

But *if* there was anyone shadowing him then, Bartlett reckoned, they would now be sitting at one of the cafes down the street from which they could observe him. He leaned back in his seat and, with incredulity and enjoyment, observed the inhabitants of the twenty-one-year-old country parading past him.

Jews from Iraq, the Yemen, Germany, Russia, Poland, Britain, America. Youthful Jews strutting with victory and self-sufficiency, more sexually aware than any young people Bartlett had seen; middle-aged and elderly Jews with indelible blue numbers on their arms and indelible suffering on their faces; preoccupied Jews wearing wide-brimmed black hats, long coats, and curly beards; Jews wearing skullcaps, sunglasses, and desert tans.

He ordered another beer and watched a bus queue swarming into a single-decker bus as if it were a captured Russian tank. A little one-armed man with a chattering face leading a gaunt giant with a ruined face from cafe to cafe selling dishcloths—everyone gave a few agora but no one took the cloths.

A smart, middle-aged woman with large soft breasts beneath white lace sat at the table next to him, ordered an ice cream and offered herself to him for 175 Israeli pounds. "Fifty dollars," she added helpfully.

"I'm English," Bartlett said. He looked at his watch. It was 11 A.M.

She took a small plastic conversion table from her handbag. "About twenty-one English pounds. And a few agora —but we won't bother about those."

"I'm sorry," Bartlett said. "It is a little early for that sort of thing."

"You English," she said. "It's never too early." She moved into a seat closer to him; she smelled faintly of spices.

Bartlett paid the old black-jacketed waiter, picked up his briefcase and started to turn left up the sidewalk. Then he

14

swivelled on his heel and ran back in the direction he had come.

At the first cafe on the right he saw the Pole in the gold-rimmed spectacles trying to disappear behind a copy of a Hebrew morning paper. At the next cafe he spotted the crewcut American attempting a similar illusion behind a copy of *Life* magazine.

At the third cafe he saw Raquel Rabinovitz.

"Shalom," she said. She was drinking a Coke through a straw.

"Shalom," he said.

"Sit down and have a drink in the Champs Elysée of Tel Aviv."

"I've already had one," he said.

"Then have another." She snapped her fingers at a waiter. Tom Bartlett sat down.

"I know it sounds farfetched," he said. "But I'm sure I'm being followed."

"It is just coincidence," she said. "You forget that Tel Aviv is just a village compared with New York or London. Every tourist comes to Dizengoff. They say it is one of the most exciting streets in the world."

Bartlett who was watching a tall Yemeni girl in a short leather skirt agreed. "But that hardly explains why my suitcase was searched."

"Perhaps an overzealous customs official opened it."

"But I had the key."

"All right—but I tell you I could open that lock with a teaspoon." She drained the Coke with a gurgle. "And I think I am right in presuming that you are not the tidiest of men. The suitcase looked to me just as you might have packed it."

Bartlett shook his head. "My wife packed it. She is a very tidy woman. That's how I know it had been searched."

"Ah." The conversation lapsed.

Bartlett considered telling her that yesterday he had overheard the President of the United States on the telephone. It seemed to him that the intercepted call might somehow be the key to the subsequent events. But he didn't want her to think he was completely out of his mind. He opened his copy of the *Jerusalem Post*.

The girl leaned across and pointed at the four young faces peering from the front page. "There," she said. "That's what it's all about."

The four soldiers had been killed in two days of artillery exchanges across the Suez Canal. Two of them at Kantara, two of them at Port Tawfik. Bartlett didn't know what to say.

"Every day," she said, "we see their faces. Alive one day, dead the next. Our young men, our future. Everyone you meet has had a relative or a friend or a neighbour killed since the truce. The world doesn't realise what those communiqués mean to us Israelis. Two killed, three injured. In a way to a small nation like Israel such figures have as much impact as the American losses in Vietnam."

"I'm sorry for you," Bartlett said. He knew it sounded inadequate. Those young faces staring at him beside news from Cape Kennedy, above an advertisement welcoming two officials from the American board of the General Israel Orphans Home for Girls, Jerusalem, to Israel. He said: "It all seems so remote sitting here in the sunshine." He swallowed the warm dregs of his beer. "Do you see any end to it?"

"Not yet," she said. "One day perhaps. When the Arabs realise that we will never be moved because the only place we can retreat to is the sea. One day when they realise how well we have treated the refugees in Gaza and elsewhere. One day when your governments leave us Jews to negotiate our own peace with the Arabs."

"One day when you give up some of the land you captured?"

She looked at him contemptuously. "What land do you suggest we give up?"

Bartlett opened his mouth to reply but he was stopped by a crack as loud as overhead thunder. He jumped. "What on earth was that?"

16

"A supersonic bang. An aircraft passing through the sound barrier. We get them all the time." Amusement softened the contempt. High above Tel Aviv, two Mirage jets headed south in the general direction of Cairo. She lit a cigarette with theatrical calm and said: "We will never give up Jerusalem, the Golan Heights, or the West Bank. Perhaps we may negotiate the return of some of the Sinai."

"You seem very hard," he said.

"All Israelis are hard. We have to be." A wisp of warm wind stirred her fringe and the sunlight found gold in the ocean depths of her eyes. "Do you realise that not so long ago you and I would have been fighting each other?"

"When the British were in occupation?"

She nodded.

"I don't think so."

"Why not?"

"Because you would have been a policewoman, not a soldier."

They walked up Dizengoff, under the dark green trees, past the police station, to the area where the small, dusky shops were crammed with sausages, matzos, humus, slabs of compressed apricots, dried fish, bottles of wine, pickled herrings and cucumbers, fat olives, halva and peta; where butchers found pork and bacon beneath bloodless steaks; where greengrocers polished and piled their peppers, apples and thick-fleshed Jaffas with pride.

They turned left down a side street where every square yellow building housed an advocate, a dentist, or a doctor. For most of the way Raquel sulked. But on the corner of Hayarkon, the seafront road, she turned swiftly and surveyed the street behind them. It was empty except for a vendor pushing a cart loaded with a glistening hillock of strawberries. The emptiness of the street seemed to placate her. "There," she said. "What did I tell you?"

Bartlett said: "I must have been mistaken." But he knew he hadn't been.

17

They walked back into town along Hayarkon. Past the Hilton Hotel, past the British Embassy sporting the grubbiest-looking Union Jack that Bartlett had ever seen. On the town beaches the young men batted balls to each other with bats like aircraft marshallers' indicators; the summer sound of ball on bat was as drowsily monotonous as the clicking of knitting needles.

Outside the Dan Hotel, Bartlett said: "Would you care to have dinner with me?"

"I don't know," she said. She stood on the steps worrying about the invitation.

"I'm an Englishman," he said. "You mustn't expect me to insist."

"I think you are laughing at me all the time."

Bartlett was contrite. "I'm sorry," he said. "I was very rude."

"I think perhaps we have a lot to talk about."

"I'm sure we have," Bartlett said.

"Like soil irrigation. And the potential of the Negev. I am looking forward to your address in Jerusalem, Mr Bartlett."

"You will be there?"

"Of course. I made arrangements to collect tickets this morning."

Bartlett took the initiative and was surprised at himself. "Then we will discuss our common interests over dinner this evening."

She smiled and Bartlett thought he detected relief that the decision had been taken from her. "Very well," she said. "But first we must see the bonfires."

"What bonfires?"

"Tomorrow is May 6, Lag Ba'Omer, a Jewish holiday, Mr Bartlett. Tonight there will be bonfires all over Tel Aviv. It is just like your Guy Fawkes night. Except that there are no fireworks."

"Very well, Miss Rabinovitz. I'll look forward to it."

"Be here at six," she said. "I'll pick you up in my car." She ran down the steps and stopped a passing sherut.

Bartlett took his key and walked past the tiny art gallery towards his ground-floor room. As he walked down the corridor his new instinct told him that he would discover that his room had been searched. His new instinct was right.

Chapter 3

The first attempt on Bartlett's life was made as he and Raquel wandered among the bonfires blazing on the bank of the narrow and muddy River Yarkon to the north of the city. Around the corner a queue formed for the Swedish film *Elvira Madigan;* from a jetty looped with fairy lights couples rowed into the gurgling, loving night; high above, the red light of an airliner moved among the thick stars.

But the children were concerned only with their fires pluming sparks and spitting with the fat venom. They roasted potatoes in their jackets, drank mineral waters and made black coffee.

Bartlett pointed to the top of one of the bonfires. "What's that?" he said.

Raquel who was wearing a dark blue trouser suit said: "It is nothing. Just some old heirloom they are burning."

Bartlett fished his spectacles from his breast pocket. "It can't be a Guy, surely."

Raquel pulled at his arm. "It is nothing, I promise you."

Barlett peered at the effigy. "He might be nothing to you," he said. "But he means a lot to a few million Egyptians. That's Nasser those kids are burning. I thought this was supposed to be some sort of religious celebration connected with the Passover."

"Just a childish prank," she said. She led him away. "For an absent-minded professor you seem to notice a lot."

20

"It's my training," he said. "Staring at rocks all the time. That's how I noticed that my room had been searched this afternoon."

"Not your suitcase again," she said.

"No," he said. "They left that alone this time." He picked up a twig smouldering at one end and lit a cigarette. "You don't believe me, do you, Miss Rabinovitz?"

"It would take more than you have so far told me to make me believe that someone is after you." She peered at him, firelight flickering on her inquisitive features. "Is there something more you should tell me, Mr Bartlett?"

"Nothing," he said.

His instinct, his reactions, and the shot all synchronised. In the darkness beyond the bonfires, in the paint-smelling waste where the skeletons of old ships yearned for the quick waters, he noticed a small shine of light like a brass knob on a black door. His instinct told him: gold-rimmed spectacles. Then a blur of face and a gleam of silver as slight as a minnow in deep water. A gun, his instinct said. He felled Raquel with one arm and hit the ground beside her. The bullet hit the fire beside them with a dusty thud.

Raquel twisted away from him. "Hey," she said. "Have you gone crazy?"

"Perhaps," he said. "You stay there."

No one seemed to have heard the shot among the cracking embers. A few children gazed in astonishment at the two of them lying on the ground. Keeping low he ran towards the edge of the darkness. But there was no one there. Although he thought he heard running footsteps and the sound of rotting wood breaking.

The girl joined him, dusting ash from her trouser suit. "And now I suppose you're going to say someone was shooting at you," she said.

"They were."

"This is getting beyond a joke."

"I entirely agree," he said. "Come on, I need a drink."

They went to an open-air cafe where men played chess

21

on black-and-white oilcloth spread on the tables. Bartlett ordered a Scotch, Raquel Rabinovitz a Carmel gin and tonic. "You're driving me to drink," she said.

"You still don't believe me?"

"I didn't hear a shot. And I can't think why anyone should be after you if your mission to Israel is so innocent." Beside them an excited chess player slapped his queen down with no respect for royalty. "What can anyone be after? Whatever it is it's not in your suitcase and it's not in your room. Perhaps it's in your briefcase. Where is your briefcase?"

"It's at the hotel," he said.

"In your room?"

"No," he said. "In the hotel safe."

"Why do you put your briefcase in the hotel safe if you've got nothing to hide?"

It was difficult to explain. A hardening determination to defeat those who were pursuing him. The excitement of a mysterious challenge as he approached middle-age after a life of preoccupation with sedimentary, metamorphic, and igneous rocks. Pure perversity. "I didn't see why they should have it all their own way," he said.

"If you're so convinced that an attempt has been made on your life why do you not tell the police?"

"Because, like you, they would not believe me."

He finished his Scotch. Down the road the bonfires were dying and the children were fishing for potatoes in the glowing ash. They gave him an idea.

"After we've had dinner," he said, "I can prove to you that someone wants to kill me."

"On your life?"

"On my life," he said.

The first course at Yunis, the open-air Arab restaurant in the ancient adjoining city of Jaffa, named after Japhet, one of Noah's sons, was served a minute after they sat down. The Arab proprietor apologised for the delay.

They sat at an unsteady table covered with oilcloth. A cat sat in the branches of a tree growing to one side of the courtyard waiting for night birds; behind them a party of exuberant Israelis in town from a border kibbutz got drunk on Coke and fizzy orange; in front of them two elderly American tourists and their wives regarded everyone with affection.

They ate humus and tehina dips with peta, hot red Turkish salad and mixed salad, and drank white Avdat wine. They had reached the barbecued fish and the second bottle of Avdat when the crewcut American came up to their table. "Pardon me for interrupting your meal," he said.

Bartlett looked up and waited. The American hesitated. Then he said: "I wasn't too sure when I first saw you come in. But I guess we were on the same plane together yesterday."

Bartlett wiped up the last of the humus with his peta. "I believe we were," he said. "And you were in Dizengoff this morning."

"I sure was. What a street that is. It's got Piccadilly and the Via Veneto licked." He paused, looking from Bartlett to Raquel and back again. "Say, do you mind if I join you in a glass of wine?"

Bartlett, who did mind, tried to appeal silently to Raquel. She said brightly: "Of course not. Please sit down." But he already had. He ordered another bottle of wine and said: "My name's Everett. Harry Everett. It's sure good to see a familiar face."

"Familiar since yesterday," Bartlett said.

Raquel said: "Are you here on vacation, Mr Everett?"

Everett shook his square, friendly face. "No, business I'm afraid. A two-day visit. That's why I've gotten myself a seat on Mr Bartlett's tour for the geologists tomorrow. So I can see some of the country before flying back to the States."

Bartlett diverted the gaze of the fish head towards another table and said: "How did you know my name, Mr Everett? How did you know I was going on a tour tomorrow? And why did you fly here from London instead of New York if, as you imply, your business is in America?"

Everett looked surprised. "Gee," he said. "Are you from the FBI?" He smiled boyishly.

"No," Bartlett said. "Are you?"

"No, sir. I'm an architect. There have been some last minute hang-ups on a new hotel my company is building out at Herzliya. I got your name from the Dan Hotel because I'm staying there too. Another coincidence I guess. Anyway I saw you walking out of the hotel today and I asked reception who you were because I thought we might get together for a drink some time. He said you were here for a conference on geology at Jerusalem. Then I remembered reading in the local paper that all you geologists were going to be taken on a tour of Israel tomorrow even though it's a holiday. So I made me a few calls and wangled myself a trip." He patted his thick chopped hair proudly.

Bartlett ran his fingers through his own untidy hair and imagined he could feel the thicker texture of the grey strands. He was aware that Everett was much nearer to Raquel's age group than he was. He decided to leave as soon as possible. He turned to Raquel. "Shall we bother with coffee?"

"Yes please," she said.

Barlett controlled his irritation. They drank Turkish coffee from thick cups while Everett talked informatively about the effect of salt and sunshine on the façades of seafront hotels in the Eastern Mediterranean. The effect was not good, Bartlett gathered, as he examined Everett's façade. A face so honest that it had to be devious, strong freckled hands, blue Brooks Brothers suit, thin tie with thin black and red stripes, square-toed black shoes. Bartlett called for the bill.

"Hey," Everett said, "at least let me pay for the wine."

Bartlett shook his head. "Buy me a drink tomorrow—at the Dead Sea."

As they walked out Everett held Bartlett's arm so that Raquel drew ahead of them. "Tom," he said as if a lifelong friendship had been crystallised into the last hour. "Can I have a chat with you later? Alone."

"What on earth for?"

"I can't tell you now. But it's very important."

Bartlett allowed his annoyance to surface. "Not tonight," he said. "As you can see I'm out with a girl. A very attractive girl. I might be in my dotage as far as you are concerned but I can assure you that it is not my intention to spend the rest of the night discussing the geological characteristics of the Beit Shean Valley with her."

But Everett's manner had changed. His fingers were tight around Bartlett's forearm and his candid, campus features were suddenly ruthless. To Bartlett the change was as frightening as suddenly glimpsing cruelty in a child. "Tonight," Everett said.

His insistence encouraged the perversity in Bartlett's nature. "I'll talk to you tomorrow on the trip," he said. "Now if you'll excuse me there's a lady waiting for me outside."

Everett's face relaxed. He replaced his mask of naïveté and patted his hair. "Okay Tom," he said. "Till tomorrow."

They walked into the street where cats waited for scraps and children waited for agora. Raquel was sitting at the wheel of her small Fiat.

As Bartlett walked towards it an old Ford V8 came rocking down the dark, narrow street. He flattened himself against the wall as it swept past.

Raquel said: "I suppose you think that was another attempt on your life."

"Not necessarily."

"I think the driver had merely been smoking."

"Smoking?"

"Hash," she said. "There's a lot of it round here."

The Ford stopped near Yunis restaurant and the Arab driver climbed out, sat on a doorstep and smiled idiotically into the darkness.

"No," Bartlett said. "I don't think he was trying to kill me. But if you drive me first to the Dan Hotel and then to the River Yarkon I'll prove to you that someone is."

First he swept away the still-warm ash. Then he began to excavate with his tools. He could smell the mud from the river and the saline breath of the sea. The girl kneeling beside him said: "Now I know you are crazy."

"Just wait," he said. "You'll see."

"See what?"

"Just wait."

It was 1 A.M. The darkness was warm, the suburb dead. After digging and scratching in the moonlight for five minutes he began to feel anxious. Perhaps he was crazy. He felt the girl's hair brush against his face. He didn't want to be proved crazy in front of her.

His trowel struck metal. "Watch carefully," he said. He dug lower and then levered the trowel upwards. The bullet came free and rolled on to the trowel. He knew how a dentist felt. "Now do you believe me?"

She nodded, her face grave in the moonlight. And Tom Bartlett found that he was happy that he had proved that someone was trying to kill him.

Chapter 4

A thrush was singing in Grosvenor Square. The morning air smelled of evaporating dew and unfurling roses and the hair of the pretty girls and young men bounced as they walked to work. But Dean Ralston, one of the senior security officers at the United States Embassy in London, was not affected by the expectancy of the morning. He walked rapidly and unhappily down the corridor of the magnificent embassy to the office of the Ambassador.

The Ambassador said: "It can't have been. There must have been a mistake."

Ralston shook his head and stared at his policeman's feet. "I'm afraid not, sir. We have indisputable proof that the Russians managed to plug into the Washington line."

The Ambassador stared grimly at the photograph of the President at his desk. "I understood that was impossible. How long do you reckon they've been tapping it?"

Ralston lit a cigarette with a large, windshielded lighter. "Not long according to my contact. A couple of days at the most."

"Who is this contact of yours?"

"Begging your pardon, sir, but I'd prefer not to say."

The Ambassador who had been accustomed to total obedience during his business life walked over to the window, fists bunched in his pockets. He was a small man with a pouchy face that belied his toughness. "What the hell are you going to do about it then?"

"The wire's been taken care of," Ralston said. "There's no sweat there. Our only worry is what information the Soviets picked up in the last couple of days. Can you help us there, sir?"

The Ambassador poured himself a glass of water. "The President has only been on the wire twice this week. Both times it was about this guy Bartlett. The President is very anxious that we gain some prestige from the four-power talks on the Middle East crisis. It seems that Bartlett can help us."

Ralston said: "I know about that, sir. We have a man out there now. The trouble is that the Russians will be on to him because of this intercepted call. My sympathies lie with this poor bastard Bartlett."

"Is there anything more we can do."

Ralston shrugged. "One of our best operators is out there. And our people in Israel have been alerted. We have an edge because we've got diplomatic recognition and can operate more freely."

"Details like that never stopped the Soviets," the Ambassador said. He tossed back his glass of water as if it were vodka.

Ralston looked out of the window at the blossoming May day. "There's just one more thing, sir," he said.

"What is it? It can't be anything worse."

"It's not exactly worse," Ralston said carefully.

"What the hell is it then?"

"It seems that one of the presidential calls got crossed. We've had a call from a local exchange down in Sussex. Apparently the call was picked up in a village down there."

The Ambassador sat down again. "You mean some yokel listened to the President talking to me?"

"Not exactly a yokel, sir."

"Who was it then?"

"Bartlett, sir. Your namesake. Apparently he was calling his wife here just as the President came through."

"This," the Ambassador said slowly, "is the sort of thing that you can never imagine happening to the Russians." He paused. "Although I guess they screw up things from time to time. Is there anything more we can do?"

"Not a lot," Ralston said. "We've already clammed up the local exchange. As far as we know the only other people who heard the President—apart from yourself and the Soviets—was Bartlett himself. Our man is on to Bartlett but of course he doesn't know yet that the KGB are on to him as well."

"What about Bartlett himself? If he overheard the conversation he must realise that he's dynamite."

"He doesn't appear to have reacted so far," Ralston said.

The Ambassador pondered on the implication. Then he said: "Hell, you don't think that Bartlett's sympathies lie in the other direction, do you? You don't think that he's a Commie?"

"I don't figure it that way," Ralston said. "He's just a geologist. A bit bumbly, a bit absorbed with his work. He probably didn't realise what he was listening to."

"How did we get this Bartlett lead in the first place?"

"Through his wife," Ralston said. "As you know, she works in the library. She has a tendency to shoot her mouth off. Normally we feed her stuff that we want her to broadcast. She's quite useful that way. But in this case she picked up the information from her husband."

"Why do you feed her information?" The Ambassador's voice was touched with sarcasm. "Of course you don't have to tell me if you don't want to. I *am* only the Ambassador."

"Because she's taken to sleeping with an Arab," Ralston said. "That poor sucker Bartlett. He's got the Americans, the Russians, the Arabs, and the Israelis on to him."

"How do you know the Israelis are on to it?" the Ambassador said.

"I don't for sure. But I'll wager a week's salary on it because the Shin Beit is the best secret service in the world."

The phone rang and the Ambassador picked it up. He put

29

his hand over the receiver and gestured to Ralston to leave the room. "It's the President," he said.

Outside the office Ralston said to himself: "And you don't want the call overheard." He smiled for the first time that morning.

From a tousled bed in an apartment just off the Kings Road, Chelsea, Helen Bartlett observed Ahmed Heykal preparing to dress. It was, she thought, a slow, exhibitionist process. His body was very brown and muscular, very hirsute; his felt cap of hair was undisturbed although they had just finished making love. She thought suddenly of the frailer body of her husband and was immediately disgusted by her infidelity. But she knew from experience that subsequent attentions from Ahmed would quickly dispel the disgust.

However, momentarily, contrition prevailed. She remembered meeting Bartlett ten years ago at a cocktail party when he had been attending a geological conference in New York. He was the sort of man who inadvertently attracted women: they always wanted to straighten his tie, remove the ball-point pen from his breast pocket; then show him the city and later their apartments. It was only during the permanent relationship of marriage that his forgetfulness and untidiness became an irritation rather than an attraction. And since he had achieved world-wide recognition in his profession they had become more remote from each other, she often staying in the town apartment while he worked in his study in Sussex. But, she thought, he was nice; she wouldn't like to think of him coming to any harm in Israel.

"Ahmed," she said.

"Yes?"

He was standing naked selecting a suit from a wardrobe like a miniature men's outfitters. In the long mirror she could see the front of Ahmed's body and, behind it, her own pale face framed with gossamer blond hair.

"Tom won't come to any harm, will he?"

30

"Why should he?" Ahmed chose a diplomatic grey light-weight and turned his attention to his ties.

"I don't know. You seemed rather excited about what I told you."

"Not excited. Just interested."

"You promise me nothing will happen to him?"

Ahmed selected a blue silk Christian Dior and moved to the dressing table to look for socks. "I promise you, my dear."

She sank back in the pillows and regarded his broad back thickened at the waist by his London cost-of-living allowance. "Why were you so interested?"

He chose a pair of black socks and returned to the bed. "It's nothing for you to worry about, my dear," he said.

Helen Bartlett decided that she was glad that Ahmed had not put any clothes on. Almost immediately the disgust and contrition evaporated.

Chapter 5

It was 7 A.M. when Bartlett awoke. A Khamsin was blowing from the south; the morning light was orange and the window was rimed with dust from the desert. Undeterred, elderly, and middle-aged American tourists were performing their exercises on the beach in front of the hotel.

Bartlett avoided the raw delights of a Jewish breakfast by telephoning for hard-boiled eggs. He lay in bed and glanced at the *Jerusalem Post*. Moshe Dayan had reported to the Cabinet on security; Mrs Golda Meir was flying to Washington to ask for more arms to balance the Russian aid flowing into the Arab countries.

At the Lag Ba'Omer celebrations at the tomb of Rabbi Shimon Bar Yohai two hundred people had been treated for insect bites, two more had suffered heart attacks, dozens of children had been lost, twenty pickpockets had been arrested and the beggars had departed with "bulging pockets." But, according to the reporter, "the spirit of merry-making was not to be dimmed."

On the Israeli-held bank of the Suez Canal an Irish captain in the United Nations had been wounded when his jeep hit a Chinese mine. The UN's task, Bartlett thought, was probably the most abortive in its history. On the front page there were two more photographs of Israeli soldiers killed at Kantara.

He switched on the radio. There had already been an artillery duel that morning 85 kilometres away on the Jordanian cease-fire line north of Jericho, and Israeli jets had attacked a radar installation across the River Jordan from Beit Shean.

On the beach outside the hotel two youths started up with bats and balls and the Americans came in for breakfast lightly coated with Khamsin dust.

Bartlett took a shower and shaved carefully with his old razor and moulting badger-hair brush. As he shaved he considered the events of the past two days. Fear, excitement, and determination to confound his pursuers fused into a single emotion. But why was *anyone* pursuing him? He decided to report to the police after the trip to the Dead Sea.

Beneath the perplexity and excitement there was another emotion. He identified it while he was dressing: it concerned Raquel Rabinovitz. The emotion was vague—affectionate, almost paternal. Paternal? He looked at himself in the wardrobe mirror and thought: "Bartlett, you're a bloody liar."

He picked up his camera and joined his group in the hotel foyer.

The geologists were assigned to five minibus sheruts visiting different destinations so that if the Arabs opened fire the world would not instantaneously be deprived of all its geological brainpower. As Bartlett had anticipated Everett was assigned to the same sherut as himself. Bartlett sat down abruptly and pulled down a geologist he had met in Los Angeles on to the seat beside him. Everett sat in front of them.

The guide was a young American immigrant named Samuel who had brought his southern drawl with him. He was dark and angular and dedicated.

"I must warn you folks," he said, "that there is a very slight element of danger in this trip. But only very slight, I assure you. There has been shooting around the Dead Sea in the past. But it's usually been early in the morning. As you may have heard on the radio our jets strafed the Arabs across the Jordan River early this morning so it's my guess that there won't be any more trouble today. Still, if there's any of you who would like to opt out now's your chance."

No one moved. In any case, Bartlett thought, you could hardly be expected to publicly affirm cowardice.

As they passed through the apartment-block suburbs of Tel Aviv, Everett turned and said: "We'll talk a little later, Bartlett."

"Perhaps," Bartlett said.

"When we stop," Everett said.

"I expect so," Barlett said.

The American geologist whose name was Wheeler said: "When I met you in Los Angeles I never guessed we'd meet here. You're an authority on these parts, aren't you?"

"Not an authority. I've been in the Sinai before. That's all."

Just outside Tel Aviv the sherut stopped at a road block. Police glanced inside and waved the driver on.

Samuel said: "Sorry folks—a necessary precaution these days, I guess."

They drove past rusting fleets of captured lorries, past orange groves and fields of sunflowers. The flat countryside began to dip and climb. Pine and cypress and green hills stepped with terraces as old as the Bible. Beside the road they saw old-fashioned armoured cars wrecked and abandoned during the 1948 war. Then new Jerusalem materialised—a wall of apartment blocks.

"The most disappointing first view in the world," Bartlett said.

Wheeler said: "At least it's not divided any more. The old and the new city, I mean. At least it's all ours."

Bartlett looked at Wheeler in surprise. He was a middle-aged man who wore loneliness like an old and familiar coat. "Are you Jewish then?" Bartlett said.

Wheeler nodded. "I never thought I'd be able to visit the old city of Jerusalem."

Everett turned round. "I understand you're all touring the old city tomorrow when you move base from Tel Aviv."

Bartlett said: "And you're coming with us?"

Everett's smile was a seal of friendship. "Sure thing," he

said. "I'm real glad I managed to hitch a lift with you guys."

"It's a pleasure," Wheeler said. Bartlett remembered the ruthlessness and said nothing.

The sherut edged round the walls of the old city and headed towards Jericho. The countryside harshened. Obelisks, pyramids, and cubes of brown and white rock sculptured and scoured by wind and sand. A few Bedouin tents like brown aphides in the distance.

Samuel said: "It was down this road, folks, that the Arabs retreated after the Six Day War." Two Israeli half-tracks mounted with machine guns crunched up the winding road; Samuel waved and the dusty, goggled soldiers waved back.

The sherut stopped behind a small hotel on the shores of the Dead Sea. The air was as dead as the sea; no wind, no birdsong.

"Kind of spookey, isn't it, folks," Samuel said. "But you see those hills over there." He pointed across the thick water at the limestone defences of Jordan. "There's as many guns in those hills as St. Peter's fish in the Sea of Galilee." He grinned proudly and pointed behind them at the brown battlements of the Israeli-occupied hills—the Wilderness of Sudan. "But I reckon there's a darn sight more there."

An ancient and theatrical Arab asked them to pose with a live camel that looked as if it had been stuffed beside a notice which said: WORLD'S LOWEST POINT. 394 MTRS. (1291 FT.) BELOW SEA LEVEL.

Samuel said: "You can have a swim, folks, if you want to. I reckon it's going to be quiet for the time being. But don't swim out too far. Just remember that the cease-fire line runs down the middle of this here sea."

In the changing room Everett said: "There's no point in dodging any more, Bartlett. We have to talk." It was an order from the man behind the friendly mask.

"In here?"

Everett looked around at the geologists changing. "No, we'll swim away from the rest of these guys." He stripped down to

35

a pair of tartan boxer trunks; Bartlett noted hard muscles beneath freckled skin. He decided not to examine his own torso in the mirror.

They walked to the edge of the sea and tested the oily water with their toes.

Samuel said: "I don't have to tell you folks not to get this stuff in your eyes. I guess you know more about these things than I do."

They all waded out and suspended themselves in the water. Rolled themselves in ball, lay out with hands behind their heads—the experts on the world's crust besporting themselves at its nadir.

Everett said: "Come on, Bartlett, we'll swim out a bit."

"All right," Bartlett said. "Let's get it over with."

"You know what all this is about, of course."

"I have no idea. All I know is that you've been following me and I was shot at yesterday."

"The hell you were. Where was that?"

"Up by the River Yarkon when all the bonfires were burning."

"Any idea who took a shot at you?"

"I think it was the Pole who was sitting beside you in the plane. But I can't be sure."

"Ah yes," Everett said. "The Pole. He's supposed to be one of you guys. A geologist." He stopped swimming and floated upright like a seahorse. "A good front. That's how the Russians work. They give a man his front when he's still a kid."

"The Russians?"

"Sure the Russians. He might be a Polish Jew but, just as sure as there are Jordanian guns trained on us at this moment, he's a Soviet agent."

"What on earth is this all about?" Bartlett peered across the motionless water towards the break in the shoreline where the River Jordan entered the lake.

"According to a message I received this morning you overheard a certain telephone call the day before yesterday. Is that correct?"

"Yes," Bartlett said. "I overheard the President of the United States." It sounded so incongruous that he laughed and swallowed a mouthful of liquid salt.

"And you still don't know what this is all about?"

"Not a clue," Bartlett said.

Everett frowned. "You're one of three things," he said. "You're either a liar, a Communist, or incredibly naïve."

"I'm going back to the shore," Bartlett said.

"Okay, okay—you're none of those things."

"I'm not sure what you are," Bartlett said. "But whatever it is you're not a diplomat."

"Okay, so my manners aren't so good. But I guess you'd better know what this is all about. Didn't you get the gist of any of the conversation you overheard?"

"Not really." How could you explain that you had been expecting to hear the voice of your unfaithful wife and that you had been overcome by an attack of hay fever?

"I suppose it's possible because you didn't overhear the conversation the day before."

"I don't listen to all the President's private conversations."

"The fact of the matter is that you can play a pretty important role in ironing out the Middle East crisis."

"Don't be ridiculous," Bartlett said.

"And bring a lot of prestige to the United . . ." He stopped himself. "To the West."

"How?"

Wheeler splashed up behind them. He was trying to do the crawl; the result was ludicrous because his body stayed on the surface of the water. "Hallo there," he said. He had already got the water in his myopic eyes and they were turning from pink to red.

Everett said: "Do you mind leaving us alone for a couple of minutes, Mr. Wheeler. We've got something rather important to discuss."

Wheeler looked surprised and hurt. "Okay," he said. "I'm sorry. I was just trying out the crawl. I've wanted to do it all my life but I usually sink."

37

"I'll join you in a minute," Bartlett said.

"You don't have to," Wheeler said, rubbing more salt in his eyes.

Everett said: "I'm sorry, Mr Wheeler."

The words were spoken by the naïve and completely spurious Everett. They were also the last words ever to be spoken by either Everett the ingenuous or Everett the devious.

In the Jordanian hills Bartlett noticed a tiny puff of grey smoke. Ahead of him a line of splashes appeared on the water and subsided. Fractionally later he heard the shots. "Hey," he said, "they're shooting at us."

Everett didn't reply. Behind Bartlett the other geologists were floundering towards the shore and Samuel was shouting at them on the stony beach. Beside him Everett floated in water dyed red by the blood pouring from a wound in his chest.

Bartlett swam up to him. But there was no pulse, no hope. On his friendly face there was an expression of mild surprise and his eyes were open just below the surface of the water. Involuntarily Bartlett put his hand on the tough stubble of Everett's hair.

Faintly he heard Samuel's voice. "For God's sake get back here you two. The bastards are shooting at us."

About fifty yards in front of him another clutch of bullets plucked the water like hailstones. He let go of Everett's body. Beneath him he felt a deep salty current. Everett's body moved away and turned over so that he looked as if he were peering at the sea bed through goggles.

"Come back, for God's sake." Samuel's shout whispered across the dead air above the Dead Sea.

On shore near the border a saloon car started up and accelerated towards Jerusalem in a ball of dust.

Bartlett started to swim after Everett's body but the current was pulling it swiftly from him. By the time Bartlett reached the beach it had crossed the cease-fire line. At least, he thought, it would never sink.

38

In his second-floor room in the Dan Hotel the Polish Jew, Matthew Yosevitz, dismantled the rifle with the telescopic sights given to him in Jaffa by agents of El Fatah and ordered a pot of tea with lemon.

Then he lay down on the bed, stared out across the placid sea draped with orange Khamsin dust and considered his predicament.

He was twenty-seven years of age, a qualified geologist with a growing international reputation, a trained assassin, an up-and-coming officer in the KGB, and a member of the Communist Party. But he was also a Jew and therein lay his predicament.

At the age of seven Yosevitz, whose parents had been killed in the war, had been taken from Warsaw to Moscow. There he was brought up as a Russian and a Communist. By the age of seventeen all traces of Semitism had ostensibly been expunged: he was a young Communist zealot and a fledgling member of the secret police. There was no treachery involved: it was merely that Communism was all he knew.

After aptitude tests held in the vaults of Lubyanka police headquarters opposite a toy shop in Moscow, Yosevitz was sent back to Warsaw to study geology and renew contacts with the Jewish community.

By these methods Communist agents were introduced into Israel as immigrants afire with Zionism. Each was schooled

39

in the attitudes to present to the Israeli screening officers. When the immigrants had satisfied the Israeli security machine the Soviets assumed that they had established an agent in Israel. And that, Yosevitz *now* knew, was where the Soviets could well be making a considerable error of judgment.

When he arrived in Israel, Yosevitz phlegmatically resolved to carry out the bidding of his KGB colonel in Warsaw. The obstacles did not appear formidable—a pleasant but ingenuous English geologist, a known American agent, and probably an Israeli operator somewhere around. But even as he drove from Lod airport to Tel Aviv the instincts of Judiasm began to awake—a heritage that could never be completely erased by any modern ideology; a heritage that suddenly germinated and blossomed on its own soil.

Yosevitz found he wanted to share the aloneness and swagger of the Israelis—but you couldn't completely discard beliefs assimilated for twenty years. He wanted to help protect his land—but he had been briefed to undermine its protection. He was a Communist and a Jew. In other words, he thought, drawing the curtains across the orange afternoon, I am a dual personality, a schizophrenic.

A waiter brought the tea. A tough-looking man in his thirties with a handsome hawkish face. He didn't look like a waiter.

Yosevitz said: "Just a minute."

The waiter stopped at the door.

"How long have you worked here as a waiter?"

"Not very long, sir. I'm just helping out. Several of the staff have had to go on reserve duty in the Army."

"Why, is there anything particular happening?" Yosevitz the spy wanted to know in case there was anything to report: Yosevitz the Jew wanted to know because of his involvement.

"Not that I know of, sir."

"Much news today?"

"Not a great deal, sir. An American businessman was shot dead in the Dead Sea."

40

Yosevitz glanced at the violin case containing his rifle. The shot had synchronised nicely with the burst of fire from the Jordanian hills. He would have to get the rifle back to Jaffa in the evening. Before the party.

"Poor bastard," Yosevitz said. He poured a cup of tea. "Can you see any end to all this?"

The waiter shrugged, powerful shoulders pushing his jacket out of shape. "Not until the terrorists stop attacking us. How can there be? And they won't stop because Nasser and Hussein aren't in control any more."

"You mean the guerrillas are dictating to the Arab leaders?"

The waiter looked quizzically at Yosevitz. "I said the terrorists. Of course they're dictating. The Lebanese are scared stiff of them. And when Hussein was away El Fatah ordered the shelling of Eilat against his wishes."

"It sounds very depressing."

The waiter said: "There will be another war. Another victory for the Jews."

"You sound as if you're looking forward to it," Yosevitz said.

The waiter opened the door. "I am a soldier," he said. "We are all soldiers." He closed the door.

Yosevitz put on his wide-lapelled jacket and tightened the knot in his thin tie. He thought of all the expensive suits and silk ties in the hotel. He looked around his fine room and thought of the poverty of the barrack-block of apartments in which he had lived when he was a student at Moscow University. Yosevitz the Communist strapped his pistol under his jacket with deliberation and picked up the violin case.

But as he left the room he glanced at a copy of the evening newspaper on the bed. At the faces of two Jewish soldiers. Both dead. Yosevitz the schizophrenic walked wearily across the busy foyer to the street. Those who noticed the pale preoccupied young man in the gold-rimmed spectacles carrying a violin case presumed that he was mentally composing.

In fact Matthew Yosevitz was debating whether or not to carry out his second killing of the day.

A hundred yards from the floodlit tourist centre of Jaffa where the most ancient history seemed to be contemporary Yosevitz sat with two Arabs in a cellar beneath a defunct brothel and listened to the Voice of El Fatah broadcast from Cairo.

Yosevitz understood a little of the broadcast. The two Arabs listened intently, talking excitedly, smoking incessantly. The voice on the radio, exhorting all refugees to rise against the Israelis who had driven them out of their homeland, stopped. A more furtive voice replaced it.

"What's he saying?" Yosevitz said. The senior of the two El Fatah agents signalled to him to be silent and lit another cigarette. An American cigarette, Yosevitz noted. The voice changed again and the Arab whose name was Hamid switched off the radio.

Yosevitz said: "Well?"

Hamid said: "It was in code. Part of it was addressed to me, Blue Lion, as I am known on these broadcasts."

Yosevitz lit an Israeli cigarette. "Was there any message for me?"

Hamid was a powerful man with greying, fuse-wire hair and a Nasser smile. "I have been told to leave the Englishman, Bartlett, to you."

"Good. That simplifies matters."

Hamid lit a new cigarette with the stub of the old. "I am not too happy about it," he said.

Yosevitz's words froze into chips of ice. "Really, why is that?"

The second Arab who possessed all the sycophany of a dirty postcard vendor shrank into the shadows of the dimly-lit cellar.

Hamid said: "Because you are a Jew."

Yosevitz took out his pistol and fitted the silencer on to the barrel. "In case it has escaped you," he said, "I am also a senior officer in the KGB. I am here as a representative of the Soviet Union to assist the Arab nations regain their heritage. Do you really wish to question my role here?"

"I do not question your ability. But it seems strange that you, a Jew, should be working for our cause."

"It is impossible to have a Russian national here since the Soviet Union broke off diplomatic relations with Israel."

"Then why not let the Arabs do your work? Our organization here has a good record. The explosion in the supermarket at Jerusalem—three hundred pounds of TNT and thirty pounds of gelignite—and the bomb at Tel Aviv bus station. All the time our organisation is gaining power."

"You *did* lose the war," Yosevitz said.

"We did not. The leaders and armies of Egypt, Jordan, and Syria lost the war. We are the true representatives of the Arab people."

Yosevitz weighed the pistol in his hand. The act of killing had never bothered him. He didn't enjoy it; it was his job— if he didn't perform the execution then someone else would. In every killing he had perpetrated, the cause had been more important than the person. At the moment Yosevitz the Jew considered the cause of Zionism more important than the life of Hamid the Arab, although he knew he wouldn't kill him. "Why then do you fight among yourselves?" he said.

Hamid spread wide his hands. "Every organisation has its disagreements." He showed his teeth—half smile, half snarl. "Even the Kremlin."

Yosevitz put down his gun and polished his spectacles. Once he had wounded a man instead of killing him because the lenses had been blurred. "Do you think you could do this job better than me?"

"It is not difficult to kill."

"There is more to this than killing. The killing is incidental." He put his spectacles on again. "What is your opinion of the National Front for the Liberation of Palestine?"

"Amateurs," Hamid said promptly.

"And you really think that you can all operate as Feda-yeem with so much disagreement among you?"

Hamid said: "El Fatah is the true voice of the Arab people. And that is what they feel." He pointed to a poster on the wall. It said: *This is the way to liberation of my homeland. And so, my brothers, I'll fight on.* Above the caption an Arab commando was disposing singlehanded of four Israeli soldiers.

The poster, Yosevitz thought, was rather pitiful. He said: "First, Hamid—to quote a Western saying—you must put your own house in order."

"No," Hamid said. "First we must drive the Israelis into the sea."

Once again instincts as old as the prophets stirred within Yosevitz. Casually he pointed the pistol at Hamid's head.

Hamid said: "There was, by the way, a personal message for you over the radio."

Yosevitz lowered the pistol. "What was it?"

"It was merely to tell you that your wife and two children were in good health and looking forward to your return to Warsaw."

Yosevitz slipped the pistol back into the shoulder holster. Sometimes, he thought, you couldn't fault the Soviet system.

He walked back to the tourist centre and caught a cab back to Tel Aviv. As the cab left behind the mosques and mildewed terraces and penetrated the neon aureole of Tel Aviv, Yosevitz the Communist sneered at such flamboyant prosperity; at the same time Yosevitz the Jew revelled in the self-sufficiency of the Promised Land.

He leaned forwards and told the driver to take him to the apartment block in Gordon Street where the party to which Bartlett had been invited was taking place.

Chapter 7

There was one bottle of whisky for the foreigners. Soft drinks and coffee for the Israelis. And on the roof terrace a huge hunk of cheese on a table.

It seemed to Bartlett that there were three main occupations at the party given by some of Raquel's friends. Dancing, necking, and arguing about politics and the Arab crisis.

That evening first reports of an Egyptian commando raid across the Canal had been broadcast. There was a suggestion that the commandos had slit the throat of sleeping Israeli soldiers; on the terrace some of the girls discussed the raid with emotion approaching hysteria.

Bartlett tried to talk to Raquel's friends but after initial pleasantries they lapsed into excited Hebrew. He felt inadequate and unhappy. He took a glass of whisky and a piece of cheese.

Raquel introduced him to an artist and an author of unspecified works. The author talked monotonously in laboured English about a revival of the stream of consciousness.

Bartlett said with spurious interest: "Have you had any of your novels published?"

The author said: "I am not interested in commercialising my art." He headed back into the crowded room where they were dancing to music from *Hair*.

Bartlett leaned against the chest-high roof wall and gazed down at the traffic far below. He had spent the afternoon making statements about the killing in the Dead Sea. He had told police about the attempt on his life the night before but they hadn't been very interested.

A detective in an open-neck white shirt who reminded Bartlett of one of the original Israeli politicians said: "Have you any proof, Mr Bartlett?"

Bartlett produced the bullet from his pocket.

The detective examined it without interest and said: "Russian."

"So?"

"Israeli is full of captured arms and ammunition. As if our young people did not have enough to cause trouble with. The other month some young soldiers robbed a petrol station with their Uzi machine guns. Last week a diamond-polishing factory was held up in Rothschild Boulevard."

Bartlett said: "I am not interested in your crime statistics. Last night an attempt was made on my life. Today an American was shot dead beside me. I believe that bullet may have been intended for me. And I don't think it was one of the bullets fired from Jordanian territory because they were grouped together in front of me."

The detective put the bullet in an envelope, put the envelope in a pink cardboard folder and wrote *Bartlett* on it. "I ask you," he said, "why should anyone want to kill you?"

"I haven't the faintest idea. Perhaps you would be kind enough to find out for me."

"We can't do much unless you can think of a motive, Mr Bartlett."

"Jealousy?"

The detective looked at him doubtfully. "Jealousy, Mr Bartlett. Why should anyone be jealous of you?"

Bartlett shrugged. "I have been out with an attractive Israeli girl. Her fiancé, perhaps?"

The detective looked amused. "I am telling you—if you go out with other men's fiancées then you must expect to get shot. It is a Mediterranean custom, you understand."

Bartlett said: "Do I really look like opposition for a hot-blooded Latin?"

The detective examined him. Finally he said: "You are different, Mr Bartlett. Our girls sometimes get a little tired of tough virile manhood."

"Thank you," Bartlett said. "Thank you very much."

"Do not be insulted, Mr Bartlett. You are an intelligent man, an attractive man, perhaps, to a certain sort of girl." He stood up to indicate that the interview was over. "And you also have manners and money that young Israeli men do not possess."

Bartlett contemplated a scathing reply. But he *did* want the police to catch his pursuers. "You'll do your best then?"

"Of course," the detective said. "Just as Scotland Yard would do its best if an Israeli in London said that an attempt had been made on his life. Although, of course, the motive for such an attempt would be rather easier to understand." He pointed at his copy of *Maariv*.

"What does it say?"

"Merely that there was an attempt to blow up the Zim shipping line office in London. Unfortunately at the moment I cannot think of any motive for an attempt on the life of a British geologist in Tel Aviv." He opened the door of his office. "Unless of course it is jealousy—and I think we can discount that. Provided of course you have told me all the truth, Mr Bartlett."

On the street below a cab pulled up and a man alighted. Another guest, Bartlett presumed. The sky was thickly smeared with stars; in the distance there was a steady drone of aircraft engines.

In the lounge Raquel was dancing with an Israeli with brown muscular arms and a lot of hair curling from the open neck of his grey woollen shirt. He had both arms round Raquel's waist. Bartlett was perturbed by a tremor of jealousy. On the wall Moshe Dayan in oils, elfin-eared and black-patched, smiled approvingly at his young lions at play.

47

The group in which Raquel had left Bartlett was discussing the behaviour of extreme orthodox Jews. During the week a gang of them had wrecked the apartment of a Jewish pathologist from the United States who had carried out post-mortems in a hospital in Israel.

A bouncy, aggressive girl said: "They are crazy people. They have no feeling for Israel. They should have all power taken from them." She cut herself a large portion of cheese and stuck it in her mouth. "Don't you agree?"

"Certainly," Bartlett said. "Of course they should."

"You don't sound very sure." Her small breasts bobbled with agitation.

"I don't know much about the ins and outs of the Jewish religion."

"You're American?"

"No, British."

"Ah," she said, as if that explained his ignorance. "My brother was killed by the British. Just after the last world war. He was trying to smuggle immigrants into Israel. You know—*Exodus* and all that."

"I've read the book," Bartlett said.

"I don't hold any of this against you," she said. "We like the British."

"I'm glad."

"We learned a lot from you."

"So did everyone," Bartlett said.

"Have you heard the news tonight?"

"About the Egyptian commando raid?"

She nodded. "Don't you worry, my friend. For every Israeli soldier killed three Egyptians will die." She sipped rapidly at her glass of fizzy orange. "I promise you." Her voice broke with emotion.

Bartlett felt very English and unemotional and inadequate. "I'm sure you will," he said.

"But it doesn't matter to you, of course."

"It does," he said. "But not as much as it matters to you."

"Are you pro-Arab?"

48

"No," he said, "I'm not."

"A lot of people in Britain are."

"A minority."

"That's not what I've read."

"I'm sorry about what you've read."

Raquel returned with her hairy-chested partner. He had a friendly white smile and shook hands as if he were gripping a bucking machine gun. "This is my very good friend Elisha," Raquel said. "He was a colonel in the Army. Now he paints. Those are some of his paintings on the wall." She pointed at a series of cubist patterns surrounding Moshe Dayan. "What do you think of them, Thomas?"

It was, he reflected, the first time she had called him by his first name. It also occurred to him that she was trying to make Elisha jealous. "They're very . . . virile," he said.

Elisha said: "What do you do, Mr Bartlett?"

"I'm a geologist," Bartlett said.

"That must be very interesting," Elisha said. Bartlett knew from experience that this observation was often the end of the conversation. He nodded and reached for the whisky bottle on a table on the terrace. The need for a second drink made him feel decadent amongst so much cheese and mineral water.

Another young man with very curly hair and curly sideburns joined them, serious and unspeaking.

Raquel said: "This is Shlomo. He is a poet. He only speaks when words come to him." Her voice became confidential. "If he does not like you he will leave."

"And if I don't like him?"

Raquel smiled suddenly. "Let's dance," she said. "They're playing an oldie."

Not so old, he thought. *Fly Me to the Moon.* He remembered dancing it once with his wife on their wedding anniversary in Churchills. Before he had realised the truth. "Is that your boy friend?" he said.

"Who, Shlomo?"

"No, Elisha."

49

Her cheek was against his. "He was once," she said. "We were on the same Kibbutz together. But you can get some very false relationships in the Kibbutzen. People are thrown together whether they like it or not."

"And you didn't like it?"

"I didn't mind it," she said. "But I didn't love him. But that was a long time ago."

He wanted to ask her if she had slept with him. But the question would be masochistic—and impertinent.

Around them couples nestled close together. Kissing, fondling, hardly moving. Watched by the one bright-painted eye of Moshe Dayan.

Raquel followed his gaze. "A great man," she said.

Bartlett nodded.

"Every girl has a photograph of him on their wall. They love him, you see."

The music changed and the aggressive girl with the agitated breasts began to dance beside them with Shlomo the poet. Shlomo moved his arms vaguely but didn't speak.

"Let's go back on the terrace," Bartlett said.

All the cheese had gone but the whisky bottle was still half full. Bartlett poured some more in his glass.

Raquel said: "You drink too much."

"Not really," Bartlett said. "But I don't feel too sure of myself here tonight."

"You don't like my friends," Raquel said dramatically.

"I don't dislike them. It's just that they're all much younger than me."

"You sound like an old man and you're not. I think your wife has made you feel older than you are. What is she like?"

"I told you once—she's beautiful."

"That tells me nothing. What sort of beauty is it? I should think she is blonde and very pale. Not the full-blooded beauty of an Israeli girl."

"I thought," Bartlett said, "that you wanted to talk about soil irrigation and the geology of the Negev."

"All right," she said. "So we will talk about soil irrigation.

But not at a party. Am I right already in my description of your wife?"

"You would be a very formidable barrister in cross-examination," Bartlett said.

"Always you try and evade the point. Am I right? Is she blonde—and anaemic?"

"She's blonde," Bartlett said.

"But you're not happy with her."

"Good grief. I didn't say that."

"But you don't deny it."

"What did you learn in America about soil irrigation?"

Raquel sighed. "You have a strange approach to women, Mr Bartlett."

"You called me Thomas just now."

"Israeli men have a much more direct approach. There is no flirtation. If a young man and a woman are attracted to each other they sleep together."

Bartlett tossed back his whisky as the generation gap inserted itself between them. A warm breeze slunk in from the darkness and rustled the leaves of a vine investigating the outside wall of the apartment. "I suppose that's the most sensible way," he said. He hoped she would say that she didn't agree with such practical courtship.

"Of course," she said, "I wasn't referring to you and me."

"Of course not," he said. He didn't know whether he was relieved or disappointed.

"Where do you go tomorrow?"

"Jerusalem—to stay. And the conference opens the day after."

"Are you scared? It seems to me that someone is determined that you should not give this address."

"Yes," Bartlett said. "I am scared. Particularly since Everett was shot this morning. The Israeli statement blames it on snipers across the border. I don't think it was. I think someone this side of the border was trying to shoot Everett or me."

"Who do you think it was?"

51

The aggressive girl joined them. "I've just met another geologist," she said. "He said he'd like to meet you."

Her companion held out his hand and said: "I am very pleased to meet you, Mr Bartlett. My name is Matthew Yosevitz."

Raquel drove her little Fiat as if it were a dodgem and stopped reluctantly at red traffic lights. Bartlett watched pedestrians, rear lamps, and headlights swerving past and wondered if Yosevitz was trying to follow them. He didn't envy him.

"What did you think of Yosevitz?" he said. He spoke elaborately because he was a little drunk.

"I tell you I do not think anything of him," Raquel said. "He is a bore."

"He is also trying to kill me," Bartlett said.

"Why should you think that?"

"He was on the aircraft. He was booked on at the last moment. He was following me in Dizengoff. I think I saw his face in the darkness by the River Yarkon. And tonight he turned up at that party. Who invited him anyway?"

"No one I think. Esther—that's the girl who was dancing with Shlomo—opened the door and he was just standing there. So, of course, she invited him in." She cut up a Peugeot taxi with accomplishment.

"Where did you learn to drive?" he said.

"In the Army," she said.

"No wonder you won the war," he said.

"I am only trying to lose this Yosevitz for you. Because you say he is trying to kill you and because I think he is a very boring man."

"Where are we going?"

"To a discotheque. So that you can see how Israelis enjoy themselves."

"I think I've seen that already."

"You can get a drink there, too. I know how you like to drink."

"I've had three whiskys," he said.

"Two too many," she said.

He put his arm in front of his face as the headlights of a bus peered into the Fiat. Then he pondered on Yosevitz.

What did he want? And what had Everett wanted? At the party Bartlett had explored Yosevitz's geological knowledge. Matthew Yosevitz *was* a young geologist whose international reputation was steadily burgeoning; but Bartlett's new awareness warned him that this man might be an imposter. It took Bartlett less than a minute to establish that the man who was pursuing him was no fake. In fact he suspected that Yosevitz's knowledge of the Precambrian crystalline rocks in the Southern Sinai and the Basaltic lava from the Miocene Age in the West was more extensive than his own. He tried him on the Middle Cretaceous limestone formations in the North but couldn't fault him.

As Raquel had suggested, the answer was probably connected with the address Bartlett was delivering to the Geological Society. But that seemed harmless enough.

Raquel parked the car as if they had stopped on the brink of a precipice. They ran across the still-busy road into a club where a Scotch cost two dollars, where bright lights stuttered, where only town criers could have competed with the juke-box music.

Bartlett waited until the records were changing and said: "What will you have?"

"A whisky, please." She looked at him challengingly.

"Are you sure?"

"There's no point in you getting drunk by yourself."

"I'm not getting drunk. Just a little tight perhaps. Do you blame me after what's happened today?"

"I don't blame you," she said. "I've been living in New York for two months and I know that many people have to drink to communicate. Here in Israel it is different. There is so much vitality that no one has to drink. That is why the drinks are so expensive—Israelis buy one and sit with it all night." She began to clap her hands to the music. "Come let's dance."

"I'm too old for that sort of dancing," he said.

She pulled at his arm. "You don't have to do anything. You talk as if you were about sixty."

Bartlett drank deeply of his Scotch and followed her on to the tiny floor. She swayed and shimmeyed, turned and twisted, while he stood self-consciously and unhappily moving his hips.

"That's very good," she said. She wore a short blue suede skirt and a floral blouse. She looked very tanned in the winking light; he felt very pale.

The explosion came as the Beatles' guitars and drums started up. The floor shook and a glass fell off a table. The music stopped.

Bartlett said: "A supersonic bang?"

Raquel shook her head. "Not at this time of night."

The shirt-sleeved young men and miniskirted girls were running for the door. The tourists stayed in their seats: explosions hadn't been mentioned in the brochures.

Raquel said: "Come on."

He followed her into the street. Together they followed the crowd running up Dizengoff.

The sidewalks were littered with daggers of broken glass and there was a smell of cordite in the warm air. They turned left up Keren Kayemet. The police and fire engines had beaten them to it.

In front of a four-storey apartment block stood the smoking wreckage of a car. All the windows in the block had gone. A man and a woman sat on the sidewalk nursing bloodied arms.

Raquel said: "You stay there—I'll find out what happened."

Bartlett stood with the crowd, sniffing the gunpowder smells, absorbing the fear and excitement that would soon be converted into hatred. There was, he thought, little hope.

Raquel ran across the arena cleared by the police. "They say the explosives were in the car," she said. "An Arab

54

must have parked it here and fled. He was probably supposed to leave it somewhere more important. I guess he lost his nerve. He also parked it outside an empty apartment block and left it to explode at a time when there was hardly anyone in the street. Thank God it is only Arabs that we have to deal with."

"Is anyone hurt badly?"

"No one. A few people were cut by flying glass. That was all. I expect they are rounding up Arab suspects already."

A press photographer took flashlight pictures.

"Associated Press," Raquel said. "I know him."

"Good grief," Bartlett said. "What a day."

She laughed suddenly and it occurred to Bartlett that he had not heard her laugh before: laughter had not seemed to be part of her insistent, inquisitive nature. He said: "What are you laughing about?"

"I am sorry."

"But what are you laughing about?"

She put her head on his shoulder and he smelled her hair and her perfume. "You must forgive me. But all of a sudden I am thinking that perhaps you think this bomb was intended for you."

Bartlett laughed without enthusiasm. "Perhaps it was," he said.

"You must not make me laugh so," she said. "It is not right at this moment. But it is good just the same. I do not think that we laugh enough."

A saloon car nosed its way into the floodlit arena. The chatter of the crowd faded. A door opened and Moshe Dayan stepped out.

Raquel said: "Isn't he wonderful?"

"He certainly got here quickly," Bartlett said.

Raquel sighed. "He is Israel's greatest security risk. Time and time they are telling him not to expose himself like this. But he takes no notice. It is not in his character, you see."

Dayan in grey slacks and white open-neck shirt talked to the police and firemen. He was smaller than Bartlett had imagined. Elf and brigand combined. Showman, warrior, and leader. Bartlett noticed that he was smiling beneath his pirate's patch and presumed that he was joking about Arab inefficiency. Dayan climbed back into the saloon and was driven away.

"Come on," Bartlett said, "let's go. I think I've had enough for one day."

She dropped him outside the Dan Hotel and kissed him swiftly on the cheek.

"Shalom," he said.

"Shalom, shalom," she said.

The little car accelerated down Hayarkon. Bartlett walked across the foyer and asked for his key.

The porter said: "Ah, Mr Bartlett. I have been worrying about you."

"Worrying? Why?"

"Because someone has been trying to persuade me to get your briefcase out of the safe. He said you had authorised him to take it out."

"I authorised no one."

The porter smiled knowingly. "I thought as much," he said.

"And you didn't give it to him?"

"Of course not, Mr Bartlett."

"Who was this man?"

"Another guest, Mr Bartlett. An American gentleman who arrived this afternoon from London."

"Thank you," Bartlett said. "Thank you very much. I'll see you before I leave."

As he walked down the corridor towards his room he wondered if it had been searched again. It hadn't. He fell asleep almost immediately.

Chapter 8

From his room in the Intercontinental Hotel, Bartlett gazed down into the walled city of Jerusalem. The strengthening morning sunlight burnished the Dome of the Rock, Islam's third holiest shrine, and somewhere among the jostling buildings, warmed the Western Wall, the Via Dolorosa and the Church of the Holy Sepulchre—the shrines of Jewry and Christianity. Jerusalem was the Koran and the Bible with Testaments old and new bound in stone. A city sacred to a billion and a half people.

And yet, Bartlett thought, the history of the city of Abraham, David, and Solomon, of Mohammed and Jesus Christ, was written in blood. Persians, Macedonians, Egyptians, Ptolemies—they had all ruled it until the Maccabean rebellion restored it to the Jews in 167 B.C.—or B.C.E. as the Jews put it. Then the Romans, the Byzantines, the Persians again, Arabs and Seljuks, Crusaders, Mongols, Mamelukes, Turks, British, Jordanians. Then, in 1967, the Jews again.

Bartlett observed from a distance and tried to be awed. He failed. The view was somehow ordained—a colour slide of Jerusalem, the Eternal City. He could hear a guide as sonorous as a psalm. It was instructional religion, a magnificent tableau, a vast crib.

He stubbed out his cigarette and turned away from the window. He had to go into the city now before cynicism took root; alone, away from the organised tour arranged

57

for the geologists. You had to feel Jerusalem, not have it explained to you Biblical chapter and verse.

He unpacked his suitcase rapidly and looked at his watch. It was 10 A.M. He had three hours before the official lunch and five hours before the conference was due to begin.

He walked along the Jericho Road and King Solomon Street. The air smelled of coffee and cedar wood. He passed a few Arab children, a donkey, a group of extreme Orthodox Jews who looked like black crows from a distance, an Egged tourist bus parked at the roadside while its tourists took snaps of a camel.

At the Damascus Gate he walked past the pleading taxi drivers into the walled city. He held his briefcase very tightly.

Bartlett took the right fork inside the gate along the Suq Khan Ez-Zeit in the Christian quarter. It seemed to him very much like any other Arab town. The alley roofs squeezing the sky, the gabbling crowds patrolling the alleys, the postcard sellers, the shops like coal cellars stuffed with sweetmeats, hot bread, wooden camels, brassware, meat moving with flies; the coffee shops, the smokers of hubble-bubble pipes, the pestilence of guides, the fighting children, the tourists as quick on the draw with their cameras as gunfighters with their guns.

One guide was more insistent than the others. A heavily built Arab in an open-neck blue shirt beneath a lightweight blue suit. Bartlett thought he looked a bit like Nasser.

"No, thank you," he said. "I don't want a guide."

The Arab caught hold of Bartlett's arm. "You will not be disappointed. Very cheap. I will show David's Tower, the pool of Bethesda where Jesus healed the cripple, the El Aqsa Mosque which was presented by the noble Saladin in 1168."

Bartlett shook his arm free. "I said no. Now clear off."

At the Church of the Holy Sepulchre belief and reverence began to assert themselves. The site of Calvary. He joined nuns and priests and sightseers in the devout darkness. Greek Orthodox, Christian Arab, Catholic, Protestant. Many with

58

different ideas about the exact siting of the Cross. But that didn't seem to matter: one God embraced the Church and perhaps the whole city.

Outside the Arab who looked like Nasser was waiting for him. "And now," he said, "I will take you to the Western Wall—or the Wailing Wall as it is called." He quoted from a guide book experiencing considerable trouble with pronunciation. "It is the age-old place of Jewish lamentation and prayer for its restoration."

"Are you implying that you brought me here to the Church of the Holy Sepulchre?"

The Arab gave his toothy dictator smile. "I am only too pleased to help."

It seemed vaguely to Bartlett that he was only acting the part of guide. "Listen here," he said. "You didn't lead me here. Nor are you leading me anywhere else. Even if you follow me right round Jerusalem you're not getting a penny. Understand?"

The Arab smiled. "This way to the Western Wall," he said.

They walked along the Bab El-Silsileh Road to the courtyard in front of the great yellow-slabbed wall. The Arab stopped on the edge of the courtyard. Bartlett took a cardboard hat from an official and went up to the wall in the section reserved for men. They stood, hands pressed against the old stone, praying, lamenting. Bartlett imagined the jubilation and emotion of the victorious Israeli troops when they saw the Wall in 1967. Again awe and reverence settled upon him.

The Arab was waiting for him on the perimeter of the courtyard. "And now," he said, "I shall show you the Dome of the Rock from which Mohammed ascended into heaven."

"You'll show me nothing," Bartlett said.

"Perhaps a cup of coffee first?"

Bartlett's reply was not in accord with the mood and the scene and he felt ashamed of it. The Arab was unperturbed.

Bartlett walked quicker without observing where he was going. The Arab walked beside him.

"If you don't clear off," Bartlett said, "I'll call the police."

The Arab smiled encouragingly. The mixture of fear and excitement that had accompanied Bartlett since the phone call in his Sussex home heightened. He walked faster; so did the Arab.

They were on high ground near the old wall of the city. Bartlett looked down and saw the green Hills of Jerusalem covered with olive trees and small, sandy houses that looked as if they could be crunched underfoot. The Arab continued to smile.

There was no one in the lane of ruined, tooth-stump houses except a few children. The Arab stretched out a hand towards Bartlett's briefcase. The smile had been erased and one hand was inside his jacket.

"What the hell's going on?" Bartlett said.

"The briefcase, please. Quickly. I have a gun here."

Bartlett began to walk away.

"Stop."

Bartlett turned and saw the Luger in the Arab's hand. He stopped. The children sensing excitement stood beside the Arab.

Bartlett said: "Can you please tell me what's going on? I've got no money in there, you know."

"I know that. Now please give it to me."

"To hell with you," Bartlett said.

"I have warned you. I intend to get it before the Russians." His finger tightened on the trigger. "Then perhaps they will stop making us feel small." He moved closer and prodded the barrel of the big pistol in Bartlett's ribs. "They say that we cannot do anything properly. I will show them. The briefcase, please."

The three ragged children watched happily; one playing with the buttons of a shirt like a pyjama jacket, another picking his nose.

Bartlett said: "You're too late. The police are here."

The Arab turned and Bartlett thought how easy it would be

to rabbit-punch him. But he was accomplished in geology not karate.

The Arab swore and turned to run. The Israeli police caught him.

One of the policemen said: "What is the trouble, sir?"

Bartlett smiled because they spoke like London policemen. Except that they wore dark peaked caps and drill shorts and shirts and they were darker than the Arab. He said: "This man was trying to steal my briefcase."

"Was he now." The senior policeman talked rapidly in Arabic then turned back to Bartlett. "He says he is merely showing you Jerusalem. He says he made no attempt to steal your briefcase. He says he thinks you have gone a little mad. The sun perhaps."

"He's a bloody liar. Do I look mad?"

The policeman shook his head. "Not really, sir. But perhaps he was trying to grab at you to show you something. These guides can be a nuisance like that."

"He was trying to steal my briefcase," Bartlett said. "What's more he's got a gun inside his jacket."

The policeman's hand strayed to his own gun. "Is that true?" he said in Arabic.

The Arab's hands fawned.

The policeman said: "He still says you're crazy."

"Then search him."

The second policeman slapped the Arab's body without any concessions to gentleness and rifled his pockets. "Nothing there," he said.

"But there must be," Bartlett said.

"Sorry sir, but there isn't." The policeman and the Arab looked up at the sun in the hot blue sky.

So did Bartlett. Was he going crazy? A persecution complex? A couple of minutes ago the Arab had been pointing a gun at him. Where was it? He looked up the road and saw the three children disappearing round the corner. "Forget it," he said.

61

He walked with the policemen through a confusion of lanes. Past ruined synagogues and living churches. There was little evidence that they were in an occupied city. Occasionally they saw other policemen and a few Israeli soldiers heavy with guns. But that was all. The preponderance of aliens among the Arabs were the tourists and the extreme Orthodox Jews, some with ginger hair and big fur hats.

They passed a sign asserting, VIRGIN MARY BORN HERE. The police left him at the corner of the Aqabat Darwish and the Via Dolorosa beside the Chapel of Flagellation near the Second Station of the Cross. He walked slowly towards the Third Station where Jesus fell for the first time. He stopped at a small hot cafe like a cave and ordered coffee. He permitted a boy to shine his shoes and searched the passing crowds for a smile like Nasser's. He felt quite calm because he was becoming accustomed to his fugitive status.

The coffee was thick and sweet. The boy's enthusiastic polishing tickled his feet. He gave him a coin and thought how much he and Helen would have enjoyed sharing the experience of Jerusalem ten years ago. Before she had settled for the cocktail values of life in preference to the afternoon-tea pleasures of being a geologist's wife. Occasionally he missed her company; but not very often these days; the infidelity had become too blatant.

He paid for his coffee and glanced at his watch. It was midday. He would have to be getting back to the hotel. He picked up the briefcase which he had kept on the table and walked into the Via Dolorosa near Our Lady of the Spasm. He was turning right towards the Church of St. Veronica when the briefcase was wrenched from his hand. He caught a glimpse of the Nasser-profile and gave chase.

As he ran he realised that he was following the rest of the Stations of the Cross up the ascent to Calvary. The Arab paused on the corner of El Beiraq and glanced behind him. Bartlett gained ground and shouted, "Stop thief." A few people stopped and looked at him with surprise. But their reactions were too slow. The Arab plunged on along the Via Dolorosa towards the site of the Gate of Judgement where Jesus fell for the second time.

Bartlett pushed and elbowed his way through the tourists, the pilgrims, the Arabs. Everyone seemed to be going in the opposite direction. Sweat poured down his face; his chest ached; his age called to him.

He lost the Arab at the Eighth Station marked by a cross on the wall of the Greek Orthodox Convent of St. Charalambos. It was also the end of the Via Dolorosa.

He saw the Arab look behind him. Then the crowds closed between them. When he reached the Station there was no sign of the Arab. Bartlett knew it was hopeless.

He walked back towards the Damascus Gate, stopping on the way for an orange mineral water and a cigarette. Before he realised it another boy was polishing one of his shoes again.

In the *mêlée* outside the Damascus Gate he climbed into a cab and told the driver to take him to the hotel.

The driver said: "You American?"

Bartlett didn't reply.

A couple of minutes later they were at the hotel. The driver said: "That will be two dollars." Bartlett again replied without respect for the setting and gave him the equivalent of fifty cents.

The geologists stood in groups in the foyer of the hotel gesticulating and talking in half a dozen languages.

Bartlett found Wheeler and said: "What the hell's going on?"

Wheeler said: "Apparently about half of the delegates went to some Arab restaurant last night and they've all got dysentery." He smiled. "Serves them right—they should have eaten Kosher."

"And what's going to happen?"

"They're postponing the conference for a couple of days.

Anyone who wants to can go home. But I'm staying—I like it here."

"So do I," Bartlett said. "With certain reservations."

"Are you going to stay?"

"Naturally," Bartlett said.

While they were talking Bartlett was paged. There was a phone call for him and it was Raquel. "Good news, I hear," she said.

"What do you mean good news? They've postponed the conference for two days."

"I know. That's what I mean. I've got to go into the Golan Heights for two days. Now you will be able to come with me."

Pleasure leaped inside him as it had in the days when he had looked forward to a weekend with Helen. "How did you know that the conference had been postponed?"

"It was on the radio. Apparently a lot of you learned gentlemen have gone down with stomach trouble. You haven't caught it, have you?"

"I nearly caught lead poisoning in old Jerusalem this morning."

"How was that?"

"It doesn't matter."

"One of your jokes, perhaps."

"Perhaps," he said.

"Then I shall come round to your hotel later today. Shalom.

"Shalom, shalom," he said.

He found Wheeler in the bar having a drink with the Polish Jew Matthew Yosevitz. Yosevitz said: "Good afternoon, Mr Bartlett. You left the party very quickly last night. It wasn't the complaint that our colleagues are suffering from, was it?"

Bartlett shook his head.

"That was a very pretty girl you were dancing with."

"Yes," Bartlett said. "She is very pretty."

"Israeli?"

"She's not Arab." He looked into the pale eyes behind the gold-rimmed spectacles. "I had quite a morning this morning."

64

"Really? What happened?"

"An Arab stole my briefcase in the Old City."

Yosevitz turned abruptly and knocked his glass of vodka off the bar. "Really?" he said. "How very distressing for you."

Chapter 9

The draught beer was good and cold and frothy. On sale, Dean Ralston decided, for the benefit of dissolute foreigners. Beside him at the sidewalk cafe of Ibn Gvirol an Air Force pilot wearing expensive green sunglasses talked earnestly to a plump soldier girl with a ponytail. They were both eating ice cream and drinking orange squash.

Ralston wiped a pencil moustache of froth from his lip and applied his mind to his assignment. Being a professional he decided first to consider his private misgivings and then file them away until the job was finished. That was the way he had worked in Saigon when his cover had been the same— magazine photographer. Instinctively his hand reached for the two 35-millimetre cameras hanging on the chair.

The girl with the ponytail smiled at him and he took her picture. The pilot did not appear to share her pleasure.

Ralston returned to his misgiving. The United States wholeheartedly backed Israel; admired their fortitude and their aggressive efficiency. But did that mean he could work in close co-operation with the Israeli secret service? Did it hell.

Ralston, who had once been a Chicago policeman and had spent the rest of his life trying not to look like one, lit a cigar and ordered another beer.

The misgivings had first been alerted during his last session with the Ambassador in London.

66

"Everett was shot dead this morning," the Ambassador had said. "You know about that of course."

Ralston nodded. "I heard about an hour ago. Poor bastard. He has a wife and two kids in London. He was due back in Washington in a couple of months."

"I am aware of that," the Ambassador said. "Everything possible is being done for them. I am deeply grieved by the whole affair."

He looked it, Ralston thought. His pouched face was very weary. "What the hell are we going to do?" Ralston said.

"You usually tell me what we're going to do in circumstances like this," the Ambassador said.

"But on this occasion you are going to tell me. Right?"

"Right," said the Ambassador. "This affair is being conducted at a higher level than usual."

"Has the President been on the wire again?"

The Ambassador poured himself a glass of water. "This morning."

"He must have called from his bed," Ralston said.

"Perhaps. He is very disturbed about the whole business. As you know he was as anxious as hell about this guy Bartlett. Then he heard that his top priority wire had been intercepted. That didn't please him any. Now this poor bastard Everett has gotten himself killed."

Ralston said: "The Israelis are saying he was killed by gunfire from the Jordanian hills. My people don't believe that."

"Neither do I," the Ambassador said. This morning he was drinking his water as if it were wine—sipping it meditatively. "My guess is that he was knocked off by an Arab marksman inside Israel. Or even a Soviet agent."

"Or perhaps they were aiming for Bartlett," Ralston said.

"I could believe that if it had been an Arab sniper. But not a KGB man." He paused. "What beats me is why your department didn't manage to get at Bartlett while he was still in this country."

Ralston said: "Because we thought we'd have a nice long cosy chat with him on the aircraft and at Tel Aviv airport. We didn't anticipate that the Soviets would have tapped the President's line and got an agent on the plane as well."

"It's one hell of a mess," the Ambassador said.

"Yes," Ralston said. He walked to the window and gazed down at Grosvenor Square. The sunshine had condensed into rain. The rain had proved too much for the small group of love-not-war demonstrators outside and they had dispersed. He lit a cigarette and waited for the inevitable.

The Ambassador said: "You asked what we were going to do."

Ralston said: "That's right, sir."

"We're sending you to Israel," the Ambassador said. "On this afternoon's plane."

"I figured you were going to say that," Ralston said.

"You don't object?"

"Not in the slightest. In any case it's not in my contract to object. But it is the first time I've been given orders by an Ambassador."

"I indicated to you the level at which we're operating. I have consulted your boss. He said you were the man for the job."

"That's very complimentary," Ralston said.

"Because you are a bachelor," the Ambassador said. He swallowed the last of his vintage water.

"Okay," Ralston said. "So no one cares if I get killed."

The Ambassador relented slightly. "He also said you were a very good operator." He fingered the small wad of flesh under his chin. "I should have thought perhaps you looked a bit too much like a policeman."

Ralston sighed. "That is my great strength," he said. "I look so much like a cop no one believes it could be true."

"Okay," the Ambassador said. "You've convinced me. Now a few words of caution. When you get to Israel you are not to have anything to do with the Israeli secret service. Do you understand?"

68

"Sure, I understand. But why? I figured we were supposed to be on the same side."

"We are," the Ambassador said. "At different levels."

"These levels," Ralston said. "All they mean is that we don't level with anyone."

The Ambassador said: "It's as simple as this, Ralston. The four powers are trying to hammer out a solution to the Middle East crisis. If we can get this dope from Bartlett we'll be able to negotiate from a position of strength. It will be great for American prestige and ultimately it will be to the advantage of the Israelis. But at the moment they won't see it that way. They want to hammer out their own solution with the Arabs."

Ralston said: "I sometimes think there wouldn't be any goddamn intrigue in the East if it wasn't for the West."

The Ambassador said: "The only compensating factor is that the Russians will be just as anxious to get the dope for themselves ahead of the Arabs for the same reasons. And I suspect they'll have screwed that up letting the Arabs in on the secret."

"That," Ralston said, "is a great consolation. All I've got to do is to get to Bartlett before the Arabs, the Russians, and the Israelis."

"That's all," the Ambassador said. He stood up and looked at Ralston doubtfully. "You really do look like a cop," he said.

"Sure," Ralston said. "Before catching the plane at Heathrow I'll check in at the precinct."

The Ambassador smiled for the first time that morning. "Good luck, officer," he said.


Ralston paid for his drinks, winked at the girl with the ponytail and walked down Ibn Gvirol towards Malkei Israel Square where he had left his hired Cortina.

He walked with long, measured strides. A tall man with big hands and big feet and a thoughtful face relieved by creases of humour at the corners of his mouth and eyes.

He had almost filed his misgivings and would shortly be able to concentrate all his attention on the assignment. But the last doubt was the biggest—the political aspects of the mission. He wished he had not been told that prestige at the four-power conference table was at stake: he would have preferred to think that the motive was a simple desire to establish peace in the Middle East. However, he did not *have* to concern himself with the political undercurrents: if he succeeded in his mission then he might be instrumental in stopping the bloodshed.

He sighed with relief. The misgiving file was closed for the time being.

He admired the square with its fountains spraying water in geometric patterns and the plastic ball decorations hanging like lanterns. Then he climbed into the Cortina parked just off the square and headed for Jerusalem.

At Ramla he gave a lift to two girl soldiers. If you were married, he thought, you could always tell your wife that you had given a lift to a couple of soldiers. Without specifying their sex.

They were very shy and spoke bad English. Nor were they prime examples of Semitic beauty. It wasn't until they were almost in Jerusalem that the girls started to talk with any animation. They were angry that coach drivers had been told not to stop for soldiers thumbing lifts. Soldiers who were only paid a few dollars a month relied on lifts, they said. Especially when they were serving in the desert.

Conversation progressed inevitably to the crisis.

"Do you think the Israelis should give up any of the territory they've captured?" Ralston said.

"Never," said one girl.

"Never," said her friend.

"There's not much hope of peace if everyone adopts that attitude."

One of the girls who was livelier than the other said: "There is not much hope of peace while the Arabs continue to shell us."

"Surely if the Israelis gave an indication that they were prepared to surrender some land there might be hope of a peaceful settlement?"

"I'm sorry," said the girl. "Could you speak a little slower."

Ralston repeated himself.

The girl said: "You may be right. But the longer this shooting continues the less the chances are. Every day opinion is becoming harder."

"It's a damn shame," Ralston said.

"Then tell the Arabs to stop shooting at us." She paused. "What can you expect us Jews to do? Ask my friend here—her fiancé was killed only a week ago already."

Ralston half-turned towards the two girls in the back seat. "I'm sorry," he said.

The second girl began to cry.

He dropped them at the junction of Yafo Road and Hanevi'im Street and drove on to the Intercontinental Hotel.

At reception he noticed a man in a dark, East European-type suit writing a cable. He wore gold-rimmed glasses and looked vaguely familiar. The man looked up and stared at Ralston for a fraction of a second. Ralston wondered where he had seen him before. Vietnam? He doubted it: it was not a face that would have fitted into the Saigon spy circuit. Berlin perhaps. Or Vienna. He might be the KGB agent seeking the same information as himself; the embassy would confirm.

Ralston noted Bartlett's room number and went to the bar to see if he was among the drinkers there. He found him having a drink with an American. There was no mistaking him—dishevelled hair touched with grey, kindly face etched with a few lines of obstinacy. He wore slacks and shirt which looked incongruous because men like Bartlett should always be wearing tweeds ballooning at the knees.

Ralston thought: you poor, innocent sonofabitch. Somewhere in the hotel there is undoubtedly a Soviet agent—probably the man in the gold-rimmed spectacles—gunning for you. Somewhere around there is an Arab trying to outsmart the Soviets to prove that there are situations they can

71

handle without screwing them up. And there has to be an Israeli taking part because it is inconceivable that the organisation that clobbered Eichmann in South America and brought him back to the Promised Land could miss out on this one.

That was three against one. Plus one Dean Ralston. Ralston sat down and crossed his long legs mounted on policeman's feet. Four on to one was bad enough anywhere in the world. But in the Eternal City of Jerusalem the unfairness of it seemed to be magnified.

Chapter 10

A scimitar moon hung over the city lacquering mosques, synagogues, and churches with placid silver. The scene was eternally peaceful. But there was no peace in the heart of Matthew Yosevitz as he walked briskly in the direction of the American Colony Hotel outside the walled city to keep an appointment with Hamid the Arab.

Although Yosevitz was divided by the conflicting calls of Communism and Zionism there was no division in his mind when he considered the business of espionage and assassination. Only total efficiency was acceptable; one agent was suspect then a whole network could collapse. And Hamid the Arab was suspect.

Yosevitz walked down the Nablus Road past the YMCA. The Walled City lay behind him. His cheap, pointed shoes looked very precise in the moonlight, his walk feline and deliberate. If he had been in charge of the operation he would not have worked with the Arabs. But his masters in Kensington and Moscow had insisted that the Arabs be consulted. Particularly the guerrillas who were now more powerful in the Middle East than kings or presidents. After all, they had said, it *is* their war. But what they had really meant was: We mustn't let them think we're trying to operate independently because we might lose their trust—and our footing in the Middle East. In other words: We must not let the Chinese in as we did in Tanzania.

As he approached the block where Hamid the Arab was waiting for him he was stopped by two patrolling Israeli policemen.

"Shalom," they said.

"Shalom," he said.

"Are you a tourist?"

"Not really—I'm here for the geological conference." He spoke in Hebrew.

They both nodded. One of them said: "You speak very good Hebrew. Perhaps you should stay in Israel. Do you like it here?"

Yosevitz said: "Very much." He answered immediately, spontaneously, truthfully.

They smiled. They reminded him of friendly New York cops on the beat. Or friendly Moscow militiamen when the frost was not too hard.

One of the policemen said: "There has been a bit of trouble inside the Old City tonight. Nothing very serious. A grenade near the Western Wall. We're checking everyone who seems to be heading away from the walled city." He looked as apologetic as a policeman ever can. "Do you have any papers with you?"

Yosevitz smiled and inwardly applauded Israeli efficiency. "My passport," he said. "And a few other credentials. I'm staying at the Intercontinental if you want to check me out."

They checked his passport and the senior of the two said: "That won't be necessary. Happy digging, Mr Yosevitz."

Hamid the Arab stubbed out the loosely rolled cylinder of hashish he had been smoking to help him forget the undignified events of the morning and listened with restraint strengthened by the marijuana to the wrath of Matthew Yosevitz.

Yosevitz said: "Why did you interfere? Tell me that, Hamid. Why?"

Hamid said: "It seemed the obvious thing to do. I should have thought that you would have organised something similar." He regarded a tray loaded with rice and mutton without enthusiasm and offered it to Yosevitz.

Yosevitz removed the tray from the small table in the apartment occupied by an Arab civil servant. "Did you act on your own initiative?"

"I did what I knew was right." Hamid gave a benign, drugged smile. "You were not there so someone had to act."

"There are more sophisticated ways of tackling such matters. It seems to me that we are working against each other."

"I do not think so." Hamid split a matchstick and began to pick his teeth. "But you must understand my position."

"What position?" Yosevitz stared angrily at the features of the Arab stupefied by hashish. First an incompetent Arab, now a drugged one. "Why did you snatch that briefcase, Hamid?"

"Will you take a smoke?"

"Of that stuff? You must be crazy."

Hamid shrugged. "So I will tell you about 'my position.' The fact is that although I do not think we are working against each other I do not feel happy about our partnership."

"And why is that, Hamid?"

"I have already told you once—because you are a Jew."

Yosevitz took off his gold-rimmed spectacles and polished them. In other circumstances Hamid would have been dead by now. Executed for disobedience, insubordination, and incompetence. Better a corpse than a liability. He polished the lenses thoroughly and put his spectacles on again. Finally he said: "I do not think they would like to hear in Amman that you have jeopardised the supply of Soviet arms by disobeying Kremlin orders."

Hamid frowned hazily. "They would not," he said. "But why a Jew to help defeat the Jews?"

"Don't bother yourself with the answer," Yosevitz said. "Now, where are the contents of the briefcase?"

Hamid carefully rolled another cigarette. His tigerish features, sleepy with marijuana, were apprehensive. "The briefcase was empty," he said.

Five minutes later Yosevitz lit a mentholated American cigarette and relaxed. The recriminations were over, his anger had spent itself: Hamid had bungled the snatch so comprehensively that he had firmly established his secondary role in their uneasy partnership. "You realise, of course, that you have scared Bartlett off," he said.

"It seems to me that he had already been scared off. Otherwise he would not have emptied his briefcase."

"That does not necessarily follow. He probably took the briefcase into the Old City to go shopping. The fact remains that the only certain way of getting this information is to capture Bartlett himself and *extract* it from him. After that we can perhaps get the papers."

"And how do you propose to do that?"

"I shall need the help of some of your colleagues across the border." Regrettable, Yosevitz thought, but unavoidable. "Bartlett is going on a tour tomorrow with the Israeli girl Rabinovitz. I have taken the precaution of discovering where they are going."

On the way back to the hotel Yosevitz again met the two Israeli policemen.

"Shalom," he said.

"Shalom, shalom," they said.

Chapter 11

From Jerusalem they drove north towards Nablus in a jeep acquired by Raquel. At Nablus they took the right fork to Beit Shean.

"There was some shelling there this morning," Raquel said. "A few Katyusha rockets. But that happens nearly every morning."

In Beit Shean entrances to the apartment blocks were sandbagged, the walls scarred. It seemed to be a hot and dull place to Bartlett.

Raquel said: "And now you must see the River Jordan."

They stopped a few miles farther on, knelt down and peered across the green valley of the Jordan—little more than a stream making its way round a windshield of cypress trees. Beyond lay the crumpled limestone hills of Jordan. Beside the road the grass was long and feathered and embroidered with yellow marguerites and crimson poppies.

Bartlett stood up to get a better view. To his right, on the Israeli-held bank of the river, he saw the snout of a tank nosing out of the bushes. In front of him, across the Jordan, there was a mound behind the cypress trees.

Raquel said: "I should get down if I were you. That mound is bristling with guns."

Bartlett got down. In the long grass he saw a quail regarding him with a bright and cynical eye.

77

They were shown round the Gesher Kibbutz by a small alert man called Dubi. The name, he said, meant Little Bear.

Bartlett said: "Were you shelled this morning?"

Little Bear smiled. "Like every morning there is some shooting. But not often do the shells reach us. Sometimes they do." He showed them the deep pock-marks in the walls of the canteen.

Raquel said: "Dubi, tell him about the mines."

Dubi shrugged. "There is not much to tell. Most nights the Arabs cross the Jordan and lay mines. We can always tell because we see footprints in the dust. But our tractors are specially protected with steel and not so many get hurt."

Raquel said: "You see, Thomas, that is the spirit of these people. They live under the barrels of the Arab guns but they will not leave."

In the shelters babies were still sleeping. On the surface two workmen were deepening the escape trench. Another was supervising the watering of the sweet peas and the cropped lawns.

Bartlett put his stock question to Dubi: "Can you see any end to it?"

Dubi said: "We must be allowed to negotiate our own peace. We have been let down before."

Bartlett was becoming accustomed to the reply.

"Are they not wonderful people?" Raquel said as they drove parallel with the River Jordan towards the Sea of Galilee.

"They are," Bartlett said. "Would you like to live on a Kibbutz?"

"No," Raquel said. "Would you?"

"No," he said.

They laughed.

They stopped at the southern tip of Galilee. Bartlett stood on a miniature Renault tank captured in the 1948 fighting and Raquel took his picture. The water was very calm and crowded by low green hills. Bartlett tried to imagine Jesus of Nazareth walking beside the water which was silver now and rippled with slight waves like fish scales. But Biblical evocations did not come easily to Bartlett the geologist.

They drove to Tiberias along the shores fringed with rushes and marguerites and placards forbidding bathing. At Tiberias the smell of sulphur from the health springs was hot in the air.

"And now," Raquel said, "we will leave Israel and visit the United States." The jeep climbed the hills at the northern end of the Sea of Galilee and stopped outside a ranch called Vered Hagalila. It was run by an American from Chicago.

They ate chicken in the basket in the bar and read the brochure. It said: *Stop over at Arab villages, dine with the Sheikh (or his assistant).*

Bartlett said: "You are a very good guide. I'm glad you were forward enough to talk to me on the plane."

"If I hadn't you wouldn't have said a word throughout the journey."

"True." Bartlett sipped his wine. "Tell me one thing, though. Why are you showing me all this?"

"Are you not interested? Am I wasting my time?"

She picked at a chicken leg. Her leonine eyes were angry.

Bartlett said: "Of course I'm interested. Don't be so touchy. But I thought you had come out to implement some of the knowledge about soil irrigation that you picked up in the United States."

"Tomorrow I shall. Today I thought I would show you something of my country. But if you are not interested . . ."

"For heaven's sake," he said. "You know I'm interested. It's the most wonderful tour I've ever had."

Outside two American tourists led their horses towards the stables. A tourist, Bartlett thought, really got his money's worth. The facilities of Texas, a Biblical background—and the possibility of dining with a sheikh or his assistant.

Raquel said: "That's all right then. I am glad that you like it. I do not know why you should question my motives."

Bartlett raised his hand. "Forget it," he said. "I'm sorry."

79

He picked out the wishbone from his basket. "Here, pull this with me."

"Why do you want me to pull the bone?"

Bartlett explained. They pulled the bone and Raquel won.

"Now wish," Bartlett said.

She closed her eyes very tightly as if she were facing her executioners.

"Have you wished?"

She nodded.

"Well, don't tell me what you wished or else it won't come true." He finished his wine and added thoughtfully: "Did it concern me?"

"Will it stop the wishing from coming true if I tell you?"

"No," Bartlett said. "Did it concern me?"

"Yes," she said. "It did."

"Ah." He watched a noble horse trotting past with a plump woman ignobly astride it. "Perhaps you will tell me when it comes true."

"Perhaps," she said. "Now I think that we should be going. I have a lot to show you."

She stood up and Bartlett observed her breasts pushing at her silk blouse. Small but effectively displayed. Thoughts which did not follow in the footsteps of Jesus began to assert themselves. He said: "Where are we staying tonight?"

"At a Kibbutz not far from here. But first I want to take you up the Golan Heights to show you just how incredible our victory was."

"I know how incredible it was," he said.

"You don't want to go?"

"Of course I want to go," he said.

They visited Mary Magdalen's birthplace and the Church of the Multiplication where you could buy a Biblical map for thirty cents and a bottle of sour wine. Then they ascended the Golan Heights pursuing the retreating white crest of Mount Hermon suspended in a mauve haze. The hills were buttered with marguerites and honeycombed with Syrian bunkers. Russian T34 tanks and armoured cars languished on the roadside, rusty and impotent.

Raquel said: "Was it not amazing how the Israelis captured these hills despite all the fortifications?"

"It was pretty clever," Bartlett said.

"In the old days the Syrians spent their time shelling the Israeli villages on the low ground. They used to kill many fishermen on Lake Kinneret—or Galilee as you call it."

They drove through Kuneitra where the Israelis had turned the Syrian Army billets into a Kibbutz and headed south again towards Rosh Pina. It was dusk when they arrived at the Kibbutz near Galilee.

Bartlett showered and changed and bought a Scotch at the tiny restaurant bar. He scruntinised the diners in case there was a glint of gold-rimmed spectacles or the flash of a Nasser smile among them. He wandered into the foyer where tourists were examining showcases of watches and jewellery. It was not his conception of communal endeavour.

He went back to the bar and ordered another Scotch. The elderly barman looked at him as if he were a drunkard. Bartlett bought him a drink and the disapproval was converted into a conspiratorial smile. Bartlett jingled the ice in his glass and tried to analyse Raquel's attitude towards him. It was difficult to believe that such a young and urgent girl could be interested physically in a geologist peering into middle-age. Nevertheless Bartlett's egotism allowed that it was possible.

He also examined his own feelings towards Raquel. The affinity was already strong and when she wasn't around he missed her. He didn't think he was in love with her: he hoped he wasn't. But there was no doubt about his desire to make love to her. Throughout his marriage he had never been unfaithful; despite Helen's accusations of infidelity and her own adultery. After ten years of marriage it would be strange to make love to another woman. And sad in a way.

Raquel joined him and ordered a dry Martini. "That's

your American Jewess ordering," she said. "Not the Israeli."
She wore a green silken dress cut low at the breast.

He said: "This isn't how I imagined life in a Kibbutz."

"This isn't like life in a Kibbutz," she said. "This is a
Kibbutz hotel for tourists. The real Kibbutz is separate."

They ordered soup and gefilte fish and chopped liver and
red Carmel wine.

Raquel said: "We seem to have passed a day without an
attempt on your life."

"The day is not over yet."

She sipped her wine. "Have you really no idea why you
were shot at?"

Again Bartlett considered telling her about the presidential call. But it would still make him sound certifiable.
"None," he said. He made his first acquaintance with gefilte
fish and decided not to prolong the relationship.

"Have you a gun, Thomas?"

"No, but I wish I'd had one with me yesterday."

"Yesterday?" she said. "What happened yesterday?"

"The Arab in the Old City. I told you about it."

She looked at him intently. "No," she said, "you haven't
told me anything. What is this about an Arab in the Old
City?"

"That's funny," he said. "I could have sworn I told you."

A dark-skinned waitress with blue-black hair brought them
the liver. She smiled at Bartlett and he smiled back. It was
certainly a friendly country, he thought.

Raquel said impatiently: "No, you told me nothing. What
happened?"

"An Arab pulled a gun on me. Luckily a couple of
Israeli police came up. But later he managed to snatch the
briefcase."

"Good God," she said. She put down her fork.

"You sound more perturbed than you were when I dug
up the bullet."

She took a drink of wine and said: "It's only that it all

82

seems so incredible." She paused. "You're so careless. Why did you let this Arab steal your briefcase?"

"It could have been worse. I could have got shot."

"You don't seem very worried about losing all your papers. You even forgot to tell me about it."

"What papers?" he said.

Her impatience lapsed into irritation. "The papers in the briefcase, of course."

"There were no papers in the briefcase. Just a copy of the *Jerusalem Post*."

Relief replaced the annoyance. "That was very clever of you, Thomas. Where did you put the papers? In the hotel safe?"

"Initially," he said.

"What do you mean, initially?"

"I put them in the hotel safe and then took them out again. It seemed to me that if there were people so intent on stealing them they would not be put off by the combination of a hotel safe."

Raquel looked at him admiringly. "You astonish me," she said. "Every day I am finding sides to your character which I never would have believed existed. It is perhaps such characteristics that helped you to win the war."

"Perhaps," he said.

"Where did you put the papers?"

Bartlett poured them more wine. "If you don't mind," he said, "I'd rather not tell you. I don't want to hurt your feelings. But I think it would be better if no one other than myself knew."

"You don't trust me?"

He put his hand over hers. "Of course I trust you. I just think it would be better that way."

She took her hand away. Her face was haughty. "Of course," she said. "I understand."

The waitress brought them coffee.

Bartlett said: "Could I have cream, please?"

Raquel said: "You seem to forget where you are, Mr Bartlett."

Their rooms were next to each other on the top of a small, one-storey block a couple of hundred yards from the restaurant. They walked across the lawn in silence. The air smelled of sweet peas and jasmine and tobacco plants. They walked up the stone stairs and stood on the verandah listening to the frogs croaking.

Finally Raquel said: "We must go to bed now. We have an early start in the morning. I want you to see El Hamma. It is a very beautiful place, I think." She pronounced the Hamma with a throaty aspirate.

"I'm looking forward to it," Bartlett said uphappily. He knew that he should take her in his arms; but he was afraid of being repulsed—as he had been afraid as a young man.

"Good night then," she said.

"Good night," he said. "It's been a wonderful day."

"I'm glad you enjoyed it. Sleep well, Thomas."

At least it was Thomas again and not Mr Bartlett. "Pleasant dreams," he said.

They lingered for a moment, then went to their rooms. As he undressed he could hear her running water next door. He washed and climbed into bed.

He listened to the frogs and wondered if she was waiting for him. He closed his eyes and waited for sleep; but his alertness seemed to intensify. He heard a light switch click and the springs of her bed creak. He looked at his watch; it was eleven. He lit a cigarette and hoped that she would hear the scrape of the match. He heard the bedsprings creak again.

When the knock came he was trembling with anticipation. He put on his dressing gown and opened the door.

"Thomas," she said. She wore a robe over her nightdress.

"Yes?" he said.

"I'm sorry I was so bad tempered. I quite understand that you don't want to tell anyone."

"Come in," he said.

She stood just inside the room and he closed the door. "It was just that I didn't want us to go to sleep bad friends," she said. "You understand?"

"I understand," he said. He slipped his arms around her and she came to him. She seemed very light and fragile for such a strong girl.

They laid on the bed and he kissed the small firm breasts.

"Thomas," she said.

"Yes?"

"You are very sweet."

But it wasn't enough to be very sweet. He removed her robe and her nightdress.

"I told you that we Israeli girls are very forward," she said.

He smiled at her and kissed her mouth and hoped that, in the peace after passion, she would not ask him where he had hidden the papers.

But she didn't. And when he awoke to find that the dawn sky was pink and pearled she was still in the bed beside him, her face innocent in sleep.

Chapter 12

They reached El Hamma at 10 A.M. Before they began the descent through the hills they were stopped by an Israeli half-track with a machine gun mounted on it.

A bronzed lieutenant with a long scar on his cheek, very white against the tan, talked to Raquel in Hebrew. She climbed back into the jeep smiling.

Bartlett said: "What did he say?"

"He said there had been some shooting during the night. Nothing much. He advised us not to show ourselves too much."

"Then why are you looking so pleased with yourself?"

"It's nothing."

"Come on," Bartlett said. "It's very bad manners to talk in your own language in front of a foreigner."

She shrugged. "He said you were a very lucky man." She leaned across and kissed him. "He was right, was he not?"

"He was," Bartlett said. He envied the lieutenant his tanned toughness. But it didn't perturb him too much; he was too occupied with his own happiness. The tufts of clouds, the sheep on the hills, the sharpness of the morning fading into heat of the day—all seemed part of his happiness.

To their right the hillside dropped steeply to the Yarmouk River and old railroad to Damascus. There were two bridges across the gorge. One had been wrecked, the other was still intact—high and noble. The sort of bridge he imagined French partisans blowing during World War II when a German ammunition train was halfway across.

The village, which had been a popular spa, was covered with the mauve confetti of jacaranda trees. The branches of the trees, still without leaves, held on tightly to the remaining blossom. In the centre of the village stood a white mosque. Nearby, the bubbling waters of a hot spring had been coaxed into a staircase of pools leading to the baths. The air smelled of rotten eggs.

Raquel said: "How do you like it?"

"It's great apart from the smell."

"It's very good for you. Behind the pools there are some very ancient ruins which should interest you very much. And across in those hills"—she pointed through the mauve filigree of jacaranda—"are the guns of the Arabs. They are most probably trained on the spa now. If you look very carefully you can see tanks over there, too. Russian ones."

They walked down beside the steaming pools to the cluster of huts that formed the spa. On the hillside above the half-track began to move. The bombardment started just as they reached the huts.

The first two shells exploded about a mile away on the side of the gorge above the bridges.

Raquel said: "I think it is only an isolated incident. They probably saw that half-track moving."

On the hills across the Yarmouk, Bartlett saw more balls of smoke and heard the slither of shells. As they exploded he felt the earth stir.

Raquel said: "It is very unusual. The officer said there had been some shelling earlier this morning. He didn't think there would be any more."

They were crouching beside one of the pools, faces close to the popping bubbles of gas. Bartlett said: "Let's get to the huts—anything's better than this smell."

Raquel said: "We will wait for a lull."

More shells exploded on the Israeli-held hills and a herd of fat-tailed sheep stampeded. They left woolly carcasses behind them.

"I'll say this for you," Bartlett said. "Your guided tours are different." He hoped that fear could not be detected in his voice.

"I did not expect this," she said.

The explosions this time had a different calibre.

Raquel nudged Bartlett. "Our boys are firing back."

The Israeli shells exploded, brief red poppies on the green slopes. The explosions rolled into thunder that found its way into the valleys and ravines. The River Yarmouk—even more of a stream than the Jordan—continued on its muddy way. Bartlett imagined the shells thudding into the green cushions of the South Downs in Sussex.

Nothing moved in the exaggerated silence after the explosions. Raquel squeezed Bartlett's arm. "Come on," she said. "Now."

"Why on earth are you whispering?"

"Come on," she said.

Ten yards from the huts they heard the whine of more shells. They lay close together looking into each other's eyes. Instinctively he moved so that his body was over hers. The shells ripped into the hillside above them.

"What are you doing?" she said.

He smiled and felt stupid. "I don't know," he said.

"Were you trying to protect me?"

"I suppose so."

She kissed him quickly, pulled at his arm and sprinted for the huts. Both sides were now firing at the same time. Bartlett wondered vaguely if the shells ever hit each other in mid-air. The explosions had merged into a continuous roar of futility.

As they reached the huts some of the ancient ruins behind them blew up. When the smoke cleared they were a little more ruined. This time the explosion was different again— vicious and spitting.

"A Katyusha rocket," Raquel said. "They might start up with mortars in a minute. They take twenty seconds to land, you know."

"That's interesting," he said. "You really are the perfect guide." He ducked as another rocket exploded among the ruins. Its blast scattered the mauve confetti of the jacaranda trees.

Keeping low, they slunk into one of the huts. "This is something I never thought I would do," he said.

"I don't suppose you did. I do not think you have much shelling in England."

"No, that." He pointed at the sign above the door. It said LADIES.

Debris clattered onto the roof of the changing rooms. Bartlett found it was becoming more difficult to maintain his calm.

Raquel said: "It looks as if we're in for quite a long exchange."

"What the devil are they shelling an old spa for?"

"Who knows why the Arabs do these things. Because they saw that half-track. Because someone important is touring their gun-sites. Or just because they've got to keep up their morale."

"I can't see that blowing a spa to smithereens is going to boost morale very much."

"It won't just be a spa on their radio. It will be a vital Israeli observation post."

Above the explosions of the shells and rockets they heard a sharp stuttering bark.

Raquel said: "Now that is unusual. A Gruyanov machine gun, I think."

"Why's that so unusual?"

She frowned. "It is not part of an ordinary artillery duel."

"What is then, then? A full-scale war?"

A row of bullets smacked into the wall. He felt their impact. He imagined them slamming him against a wall, shattering bone and flesh. His hands and lips were trembling.

He found Raquel's hand and held it and was reassured to find that she, too, was shivering. He didn't speak because he didn't want her to hear the fear in his voice.

The machine gun stopped. And the rockets. Only the shells continued whining overhead, wounding the hills beyond and killing the sheep.

Raquel squeezed his hand. "Thomas."

"Yes?"

"I'm scared."

He pressed her hand without replying. He thought he heard a sound in another of the changing rooms. But it was probably a broken window moving in the blast from the explosions.

The door was kicked open as Bartlett was sitting up. There were three of them. Two were pointing submachine-guns, the third held a Kalatchnikov automatic rifle. They wore black and white cloths around their heads and grenades in their belts.

The Arab with the rifle frisked them.

Bartlett said: "What the hell is this all about?" It sounded completely inadequate. His voice was dry with fear.

"You will understand later," said the Arab with the rifle who was the leader. "Now we must be quick. You must come with us."

"Who the hell are you?"

"El Fatah," said the Arab.

"Where are you taking us?"

"Across the river while the shelling is still going on. Please —come with us." He jerked the rifle.

"Both of us?"

"No, just you. The girl must stay here."

He spoke such good English that he might have been a diplomat.

Bartlett said: "What's going to happen to her?"

"You need not bother yourself about that."

One of the Arabs armed with a submachine gun approached Raquel. She hit him in the face with a small, white-knuckled fist. Blood trickled from one of his nostrils.

The El Fatah leader said: "That was very foolish. He was only going to tie you up. Please tell her to co-operate, Mr Bartlett."

"How did you know my name?"

"It does not matter. Now put your hands up and walk in front of me."

"I'm not going anywhere without the girl."

The Arab slung the rifle over his shoulder and drew a pistol. He rammed the barrel into Bartlett's back. "I'm afraid you are, Mr Bartlett. Now move."

Bartlett considered swinging round and hitting him across the throat with the side of his hand. But even if it worked it wouldn't divert the bullets of the two submachine guns. He moved towards the open door.

He was through the door leading into a lounge when there was a blur of movement beside him. He saw an arm raised and heard it chop on to the El Fatah leader's neck. The Arab moaned, dropped his pistol and pitched forward. A hand grabbed Bartlett and pulled him to one side. As Bartlett jerked sideways one of the other Arabs fired a burst from his submachine gun. The explosions in the confined space hurt the eardrums; the bullets ricocheted round the room smashing windows and fracturing a water pipe.

The newcomer who had an American accent said: "You stay here. Distract their attention. I'm going round the back." He took the Arab's pistol, crawled across the floor and disappeared outside the building.

Raquel shouted to Bartlett from the changing room. "Are you all right?"

"I'm okay," he said. "What about you?"

"I'm all right."

One of the Arabs spoke in very bad English. "Drop all your weapons and come back here. We have the girl."

"Take no notice," Raquel said. "Try and get back to that half-track and let them know what's happening."

One of the Arabs fired a burst into the ceiling above the door. The ferocity of the impact scared Bartlett. Chunks of plaster fell around him. "I'll have to give myself up," he said. "They'll shoot you if I don't."

"If you do I'll never respect you again," she said.

One of the Arabs said slowly: "You must come in here now. If you do not then we shall kill the girl."

"I'm coming," Bartlett said.

Through a broken window he saw flame and smoke blossoming on the hillside. By this time the American must surely be somewhere behind the Arabs.

Another clutch of bullets slammed into the ceiling.

One of the Arabs said: "This is your last chance. If you do not come we shoot the Israeli girl."

"Just a minute."

"What is the matter?"

Bartlett didn't know what the matter was. Then he heard the American's voice: "Drop those guns." Bartlett peered round the corner. The American was at the window with the pistol levelled at the two Arabs. He said again: "Drop those guns. Now. Or I'll shoot." He jerked the pistol at them.

One of the Arabs turned, pressing the trigger of the machine gun as he moved. But the American's pistol fired first. The machine-gun bullets punctured a line of holes in the wall and smashed a cistern in a toilet. The Arab clutched his side and slumped on to the ground on top of his gun.

The American said to the other Arab: "And now you. Drop that machine gun. And any other weapons you've got."

The Arab said: "This is all I have got." He turned slowly and deliberately and squeezed the trigger. The bullets smashed the remaining fragments of glass in the window. But the American had ducked before the Arab fired.

Without really thinking what he was doing Bartlett grabbed the Arab from behind. He smelled sweat and cordite and felt the springed power of the man beneath his camouflaged combat jacket. He knew he could only hold him briefly.

The Arab stabbed backwards with the butt of the submachine gun. It hit Bartlett just below the sternum. His legs were folding and he wanted to vomit. But he held on to the Arab's throat with the crook of his arm.

The American vaulted through the window. The Arab pressed the trigger once more but Bartlett had spoiled his aim. Water gushed from a washbasin shattered by the bullets. The American clubbed him on the temple with the butt of the pistol and all was quiet in the ladies' changing room except for the reverberations of the gunfire outside and the sound of escaping water.

Finally the American said: "Boy, oh boy."

Raquel was cradling Bartlett's head and stroking his hair. "You were wonderful," she said.

The American said: "He sure was." He examined the Arab leader. "He'll live," he said. "But he'll need some waking." He moved the second Arab's body with his foot. "He's dead." He looked at the third. "He's waking up already." He kicked the submachine gun away and removed the grenades and another pistol tucked inside the combat jacket. "I guess we'd better tie him up." He looked around. "Is there any rope or anything around?" He looked around and went to the closet. "I reckon we'll just have to improvise," he said. He ripped down the chain and bound the waking Arab's hands with it.

Raquel said: "I think we will be waiting here for a long time. The Arabs started shelling so that these men could get across the river. They will be waiting for them to return."

"I seem to be the most wanted man in the Middle East," Bartlett said.

The American said: "Just out of interest, what the hell is all this about?"

"Just out of interest," Bartlett said, "what were you doing outside the changing rooms?"

"I just came up here on a visit. I'm a photographer, by the way. Name of Ralston. Dean Ralston. I work for a magazine in the States." He got up from one of the benches in the lounge and shook their hands.

"But why did you choose El Hamma?" Raquel said.

93

Outside the gunfire was becoming spasmodic.

Ralston said: "It's got everything a photographer needs. Colour, spectacular scenery. A mosque and a spa. It's God's gift to a cameraman, Mr Bartlett. Especially if you're lucky enough to get any action. And we've sure had that."

Bartlett said: "And you just happened to be standing here when the Arabs set on us."

"Not exactly." Ralston struck a match on the sole of his big shoe and lit a cigar. "I saw you arrive and walk down beside the sulphur springs just as the shelling started. I saw you heading for these huts and figured that was a good idea. Then I saw these guys running like hell from the direction of the river. So I hid behind the door. I was just wondering what to do when one of them marched you through the door right in front of me." He checked that his cigar was burning evenly. "Now you tell me what this was all about."

"I wish I knew," Bartlett said.

"And you, ma'am. Do you know what they were up to? I guess they wanted you as a hostage or something. Perhaps they thought your friend here was an Israeli general." He glanced at Bartlett. "No, I guess not. He doesn't really look like an Israeli let alone a general."

Bartlett hunched forward, elbows on knees. His stomach hurt and he felt sick. He lit a cigarette and coughed violently. "The shelling has almost stopped," he said. "I think we can go."

They waited another five minutes. Bartlett stood up wearily. "Come on," he said, "let's go."

The American told the manacled Arab to get up. He stuck the pistol in his back and marched him out of the changing rooms. Bartlett and Raquel walked behind. Bartlett thought that Ralston looked like a policeman. So much like a policeman that he couldn't possibly be one. Or could he? Bartlett didn't know any more.

Raquel drove with her foot pushed hard down on the accelerator. Ralston's fawn Cortina began to drop back.

Halfway up the hill they came to the half-track. It had been blown off the road by a shell. Already they were taking the wounded away by ambulance. But the faces of two of the soldiers on the stretchers were covered with blankets.

Raquel stopped the car and spoke to one of the soldiers sitting on the verge. He was smoking a cigarette and his face was dazed and dirty.

Bartlett asked the ambulance men if there was anything they could do. But there wasn't.

The road was littered with metal and equipment and jagged daggers of shell-casing.

Raquel came back. "The lieutenant," she said. "He's dead."

She let out the clutch and they moved off past the ambulance.

"I'm sorry," Bartlett said. And was aware once more of his inadequacy in such matters. "Would you like me to drive?"

She shook her head and brushed the tears from her eyes with her hand. "No, I would rather drive."

As the jeep sped towards Galilee, Bartlett remembered the insignificant statistics he used to see in the British newspapers. "Two dead, three injured." Tomorrow, he thought, he would see the face of the young lieutenant staring out from the front page of the morning newspaper.

Chapter 13

The situation, Ralston decided, was not without its ironies. Instead of persuading Bartlett to part with information he had rescued him and was now about to dine with him. And his Israeli girl friend and the girl friend's formidable mother.

From the balcony of the Rabinovitz fifth-floor apartment Ralston stared over the Sabbath-silent city of Tel Aviv to which they had returned for dinner. No shops open, few taxis, few people; no booze. But with the first star life would start up again with frenetic desire to recoup for a lost day— or so it seemed to a Gentile. The boulevard cafes would be packed, each with its own kind—artists or authors, old or young, Jews of German or Russian or American descent. Cinemas and theatres were already booked up for the evening. The streets would be thronged with a babel of nationalities; at a thousand parties they would be wooing and warring and forming another political party or two.

Ralston gazed across the cubes of apartment blocks and the green-lined boulevards past the Shalom Mayer Tower, towards the sea. The action that morning seemed very remote in the studied peace of the Sabbath. He wished he was collaborating with these people instead of serving political prestige.

He picked up an Israeli magazine lying on a wickerwork chair. There was a lot about the Zionist organisations in the States in it. A long article about the United Jewish Appeal.

An advertisement inserted by the United Israel Appeal inviting members to a special session of the Zionist General Council. An announcement about the appointment of officials at the Israel-America Society's Haifa branch. An invitation from the Jewish National Fund to plant trees in the Hills of Judea.

Ralston's appreciation of the bonds uniting America and Israel strengthened. And, as dusk approached, he opened up the file once more on Misgivings about the Assignment. Ten minutes later he had almost persuaded himself again that if his efforts contributed to peace then subsidiary considerations didn't matter. And it would certainly be a blow against Communism if the West in the shape of the United States managed to produce the formula that would ensure that peace. Would it be so bad if the United States did gain a little prestige to counter her critics? Ralston decided it wouldn't. But he was glad that he wasn't an American Jew in Israel because then he wouldn't be sure where his loyalties lay.

A winking aircraft flew across the sky which was losing the lustre of the day. Beneath the balcony a couple of cars pulled out from the kerb. He dropped his glowing cigar butt and watched it spin down to the lawn.

Then he considered his quarry. Was Bartlett a mug? Ralston didn't think so. He was sufficiently acquainted with British agents to know that they were accomplished actors—particularly when portraying amicable eccentrics. But that didn't mean he was convinced that Bartlett *was* an agent. It was possible that he might be; but if he was he was decidedly overplaying the amiable eccentric. And he seemed to have no positive affiliation to Arab or Israeli, to the Western or Communist powers.

Ralston lit another cigar and looked for the first star in the green sky. Nothing.

But if Bartlett was the complete innocent why had he gone to such extremes to hide the contents of his briefcase? This aspect of the operation grieved Ralston; he drew deeply on his cigar and exhaled a long, aggressive jet of smoke. First

97

the porter at the Dan had treated his forged note of authority with contempt–the contempt it deserved, Ralston admitted. Then Bartlett had wandered into the walled city with a briefcase full of nothing. Now—as far as could be ascertained— he had hidden the contents somewhere in Jersualem. There could be only one answer: Bartlett had understood the conversation between the President and the Ambassador in London.

So what could be done about it?

Bartlett said: "Shabbat, shalom."

Ralston turned round. "Shalom," he said.

Bartlett gave his slow, friendly smile. "I understand that on the Sabbath you say Shabbat, shalom."

Ralston grinned despite his problems. "Hi," he said.


The dinner was very good. After Martinis there was paté; then steaks and mixed salad and French fries, a lot of local red wine and some sharp salty cheese. Ralston noticed no concessions to Kosher.

Raquel's mother, who was inclined to plumpness, with curly auburn hair that could have been dyed, said: "We are good Jews in this household. But we do not follow the dietary rules as strictly as we should. Not so many Israelis do these days."

Ralston sipped his wine and tried to assess the relationship between Bartlett and the girl. Meeting a Jewish girl's mother was not a step to be undertaken lightly. But perhaps Bartlett's intentions were platonic; anything was possible with such a man. If Ralston had been touring Israel and the occupied territories with Raquel the spirit of Plato would not have been in evidence. But Ralston sympathised with Bartlett whatever his intentions were—because he had met Bartlett's wife.

Mrs Rabinovitz said: "I think you are looking very thoughtful, Mr Ralston."

"It's enough to make one thoughtful," Ralston said. "This hospitality and this food and this company."

"I'm glad that you like it," she said. Her accent was Brooklyn, Russian, Jewish—any accent you liked to put on the label. Her tone was gentle but assertive and would always call to order her daughter's occasional indiscretions.

By the time they had reached the meat course politics and religion had been disposed of and the conversation had inevitably reached the Arab crisis.

Ralston sliced into his tender steak and said: "I have a theory about how the Israelis could conquer all the Arab countries."

"Is that right?" Raquel said. "Then I am sure Moshe Dayan would be very pleased to hear it." She glanced at the photograph of the Defence Minister on the wall.

Mrs Rabinovitz said: "Tell us about your theory, Mr Ralston."

"It's like this," Ralston said. "Since coming to your country I have attempted to get across the road on a pedestrian crossing. I have also tried to get served at a post office. I reckon both are pretty frightening experiences. Now if you could paint pedestrian crossings right round your country's borders it would ensure that all Israeli motorists would drive straight across them without bothering to see if anyone was on them."

Mrs Rabinovitz chuckled. "And what about the post office —how does that figure in this ingenious theory of yours, Mr Ralston?"

"Not the post office itself, Mrs Rabinovitz. The customers. It is my theory that Israelis trying to fight their way to the counter are the best shock troops in the world. Put them into the attack after the motorists and you could take Cairo tomorrow."

The two women laughed; Bartlett smiled remotely. Raquel put her hand on his arm. "Thomas," she said, "you do not seem very happy this evening."

"I'm sorry," he said.

Mrs Rabinovitz said: "Perhaps Shabbat has been too much for Mr Bartlett."

Raquel said defensively: "You seem to forget that he was

nearly captured by the Arabs and that one of them stuck a machine gun butt in his stomach."

"It's not that so much," Bartlett said. "It's just all that unnecessary death and suffering."

Raquel withdrew her hand. "You mean the deaths of the Israeli soldiers?"

Bartlett nodded. "And the Arab."

Raquel said: "If Mr Ralston had not shot him he would have killed us. I ask you, how can you sympathise with El Fatah?"

"They were brave men," Bartlett said.

No one spoke. The only sound was the scrape of knife and fork on plate. The light from the candles on the long table made their faces holy.

Finally Raquel said: "They were terrorists."

Ralston wondered again about Bartlett's affinities.

Mrs Rabinovitz said: "Terrorists they might have been. But Mr Bartlett is right—they were brave. Both sides have brave men. It is sad that so much bravery should go to waste."

Raquel said: "I do not remember so much bravery from the Arabs during the war."

"Then you are a very silly girl," Mrs Rabinovitz said. "There was much bravery on both sides."

Bartlett sipped absent-mindedly at his wine. "It is the young people of Israel who frighten me. They are so aggressive, so reluctant to accept any point of view other than their own."

Ralston said: "Isn't that true of young people anywhere in the world?"

"They aren't fighting a war," Bartlett said.

Mrs Rabinovitz said: "I do not think that you should worry yourself too much, Mr Bartlett. Israel is not governed by its youth. In Mrs Meir we have a wonderful leader. But as we are discussing youth then it is the youth of the Arab countries who should alarm you. El Fatah, the National Front for the Liberation of Palestine. It is they who are the fanatics al-

100

ready. And they are beyond the control of their countries' leaders."

Raquel said sulkily: "But they are all very brave, are they not, Mr Bartlett?"

Mrs Rabinovitz said: "Do not be stupid, Raquel."

Ralston consulted his watch. "The news in English," he said. "Let's have the radio on."

They listened to the impersonal woman's voice describe the incident at El Hamma. An artillery duel. Two Israeli soldiers killed, three wounded. There was no mention of Ralston or Bartlett or Raquel.

Ralston said: "I guess they don't want to suggest that there was any American intervention." He grinned to show that he was joking because the atmosphere was not sympathetic to humour.

Raquel said: "We'll have coffee on the verandah."

Ralston sat in the wicker chair opposite Raquel and Bartlett while Mrs Rabinovitz made coffee in the kitchen. Tel Aviv was alive again. In a nearby apartment he heard laughter and singing. The sidewalks were moving with people, the streets weaving with cars.

Raquel sat close to Bartlett and said: "I'm sorry."

Bartlett patted her hand paternally and said: "That's all right."

"I realise that the Arabs were brave."

"If everyone could make concessions like that there might be some hope for peace."

Raquel nodded and put her head on his shoulder.

Watching her face in the candlelight from the dining room Ralston decided that she was either in love with Bartlett or she was a superb actress. It was at this point that he also decided she was an Israeli agent.

Chapter 14

Raquel Rabinovitz parked her Fiat near the press office in Tel Aviv and walked briskly up Kaplan Street past the Ministry of Defence. Outside the Ministry the street was busy with uniforms. She saw an Air Force officer walking with a girl soldier and exalted in the classlessness of Israeli society. She remembered how, during her Army service in the Sinai, she had heard noncommissioned men talking to generals as if they were equals. Nowhere else in the world could such relationships exist; but nowhere else in the world was the motive for military service so unified: private and general were both fighting for survival.

The morning was heating up. A few tourists were out hoping to see Moshe Dayan arriving at his ministry; traffic was building up and making pedestrians jump on the crossings. Raquel turned right down Bet Street and headed for the office which had nothing to do with soil irrigation.

Her thoughts turned, as they turned most days, to the man she had been going to marry. Medium height, shortish hair, green eyes, inclined to be histrionically tough, but really very gentle. He had once risked disciplinary action for refusing to demolish one of five Arab homes that were to be destroyed in Gaza as retaliation for terrorism because the family inside was sick; when his commander had seen the family he had agreed. Tough and gentle and dead for more than a year. Killed by a grenade thrown by a terrorist.

She felt the wallet in her pocket that still contained his photograph. Since the day he had been killed patriotism and a desire for revenge had fused into one emotion. Now her feelings were confused by the presence of Bartlett. She wished in a way that she had not been available to carry out the instructions to get to know him.

Since the death of her fiancé she had not slept with another man. Not until the other night with Bartlett. She was still surprised how natural it had been to make love to him. Because outwardly he did not possess any of the qualities which she had always looked for in a man. In particular he lacked the aggressiveness which Israeli women tended to admire.

She saw him with his arm crooked round the El Fatah gunman's neck; she saw the machine-gun butt jabbing into his stomach. She felt his pain and inwardly cried out for him. And she knew she loved him for his courage which was not packaged in muscled belligerence, for his kindness and even his vagueness.

She turned into an alley where thin cats, some with two eyes and some with one, scavenged and fought and copulated with the intensity of the doomed. She walked up an iron staircase and opened a door marked F. FRISHMAN—FUNERALS ARRANGED AND EXECUTED. It was, she thought, most apt.

Julius Peytan spoke Hebrew with a South African accent. Occasionally he lapsed into English or Yiddish or his native Afrikaans. His linguistics could have been confusing, but he spoke with such deliberation and controlled power that his message was communicated whatever the language.

He was a large broad man with pillows of muscles just beginning to go slack. He wore dark trousers and an open-neck white shirt riding loose around his navel. He smoked a lot with the same deliberation that he talked—tasting the smoke, inhaling deeply, crushing out the butts with finality. His face was heavy featured, a little jowelly, and his eyes were the colour of the smoke that trickled from his cigarettes. But whereas the smoke had warmth there was none in the eyes of Julius Peytan.

He had come to Palestine from Johannesburg in the '30s and had rapidly ascended the hierarchy of the Haganah. He had been imprisoned by the British and still harboured a certain admiration for those who had caught him because he had been deceived by their apparent naïveté. He had studied British methods and incorporated them in his own textbook of skills. After independence he had concerned himself with the pursuit of Nazis who had fled from their atrocities. As a result he knew South America as well as his native South Africa. Another result was promotion to the hierarchy of the Israeli secret service, the Shin Beit.

He leaned back now in his creaking swivel chair that seemed inadequate for his size and listened to Raquel Rabinovitz. The room was hardly furnished at all—chair and desk, a bookshelf nailed to the wall, a lot of maps, photographs of Israeli political leaders. On the table was a blotter, a pack of cigarettes, a box of matches, and a Smith & Wesson.

Raquel's words dwindled and died. They usually did when she was confronted by his impassive concentration.

Peytan said: "What are you trying to tell me, Miss Rabinovitz?"

"Have I not made myself clear already?"

He shook his head slowly. "Please go through it again." He ground out a cigarette as if he were squashing an insect.

"Look, I do not like this assignment," Raquel said. "I have no heart for it. I know this should have no bearing on it. But really it is for the sake of Israel that I have come to see you because I cannot do my job properly."

Peytan lit another cigarette and inhaled hugely. "You surprise me, Miss Rabinovitz. You have always struck me as possessing greater strengths than the average woman. That is precisely why you were chosen for this assignment. You do not need me to remind you of the importance of this assignment to Israel."

There was a hint of menace in his voice. "I know of its importance," she said. "That is why I am thinking that you should assign someone else to the job."

Peytan considered and analysed the statement. Then he said: "There is no one else, Miss Rabinovitz."

"But you have other women agents."

"It is too late. Far too late. You have made contact with Bartlett. You must finish the assignment." He paused. "In fact, I am surprised that you have not completed it already. After all, you have slept with him, have you not?"

Raquel blushed and was angry with herself because the blush betrayed feminine frailty. "Have you been keeping me under observation?"

"No. I am merely presuming that you have slept with him because you are a capable operator. You have the advantage there over Yosevitz."

Raquel looked at the Smith & Wesson and imagined its barrel stabbing into the spine of a fugitive Nazi. "This man Yosevitz," she said. "Why have you not done anything about him?"

Peytan stared at his cigarette: it looked like a matchstick in his large freckled hand. "He is, after all, a Jew," he said.

"And an enemy of Israel."

"Yosevitz is an interesting case. I have known many men sent in by the Russians under the guise of immigrants for the purpose of subversion. Usually they have failed because the men themselves soon realise their true destiny."

"What if none of this applies to Yosevitz? What if he succeeds in this mission?"

Peytan lifted his bulk from the chair and patrolled the room. For a man of his size he was surprisingly light-footed.

Raquel looked at him warily. "Well," she said, "what would happen?"

Peytan stopped in front of a wall map showing the 1967 cease-fire boundaries. "He would be killed, of course," he said.

"But what if he managed to communicate the information to the Arabs?"

"The answer to that is very simple," Peytan said. "He wouldn't communicate it to the Arabs. The Russians want it for themselves. They want to negotiate the Middle East peace themselves. You see, at the moment they are just gun-runners to the Arabs. They want more power, more prestige. Just as our friends the Americans want to be the peacemakers. But the Russians have even more at stake: they want to keep the Chinese out." He lit another cigarette with deliberation. "These days we are finding that more and more Chinese weapons are being used by the Arabs."

Raquel said: "It sounds very complicated."

Peytan shrugged. "This is the Middle East. The Levant. Immediately anyone becomes involved with us then their lives become complicated."

"What about Ralston?" Raquel said.

"Ah yes, Ralston." Peytan sat down again in the creaking chair. "We are not absolutely sure about Mr. Ralston. But the weight of evidence would indicate that he is working for American intelligence. We must presume that he is the successor to Everett."

"There is *no* doubt," Raquel said. "Look, was it just coincidence that he turned up at El Hamma?"

"I agree." A tiny smile thawed on his face. "But you, Miss Rabinovitz, have a distinct advantage over Mr Ralston."

"I have told you—I do not think I can operate as well as I should."

"Are you in love with Bartlett?"

Raquel glanced into her handbag lying open on her lap and saw the picture of her dead fiancé looking up at her from her wallet. "I don't know," she said.

"I think you are. It astonishes me because I cannot see the attraction of a man like Bartlett to a girl like you. But then it would not be the first time that the qualities of the British have surprised me. However, Miss Rabinovitz, that is beside the point. Your country comes before everything. I think you would agree with that?"

Raquel nodded.

"And after all there is not much future for you with such a man. He is not, after all, a Jew. And he is also married."

"I know. But you cannot control these things."

"Poor man. That he should have such a wife."

Raquel looked at him with fresh interest. "You know Bartlett's wife?"

"I know of her."

"What is she like?"

Peytan shook the last cigarette out of the pack. "She has a big mouth," he said.

"Is that all you know?"

"She has provided us with quite a lot of information in the past. At cocktail parties and so on. But evidently the Americans also appreciated her worth because these days most of the information is false."

"Except this information?"

Peytan nodded. "But she didn't get this from the Americans. She got it from her husband—the poor dumb bastard."

Raquel said tautly: "He is not dumb."

Peytan held up his hands but the gesture did not make him appear defenceless. "Okay. He's a highly intelligent man already—he must be if he's a geologist. But he is, perhaps, a little naïve."

"He is not naïve. It is just that he knows nothing about your sort of business."

"Or yours," Peytan said.

"All right," she said. "Or mine."

Peytan's voice hardened. "Now I think we understand each other, Miss Rabinovitz. You know your assignment and I expect you to carry it out regardless of any sentimental attachments you may have formed. I expect you to do this for the sake of your country and your people. Is that understood?"

She nodded. "It's understood."

"Then please return to your duties. Time is running short."

"You know he's hidden the contents of the briefcase?"

"It should not be difficult for a girl of your accomplishment to find the hiding place."

She stood up and snapped her handbag shut. "That was an unpleasant remark to make." She was surprised at her spirit.

He said: "In this business we do not take too much heed of the pleasantries, Miss Rabinovitz." He screwed up the empty cigarette pack and threw it on the floor. The interview was over.

She walked slowly back to her car. She felt the sun's warmth on her shoulders; the streets were crowded with soldiers—and the civilians they were defending; there was vibrancy in the air and vitality in the people. Men looked at her with admiration, women with envy. But Raquel Rabinovitz revelled in none of it.

She climbed into her baby car and drove to the seafront restaurant where Bartlett was waiting for her. It was one of the cafes frequented by prostitutes who specialised in hauling surprised tourists off the sidewalk. When they were not soliciting with characteristic Israeli determination they sat knitting.

One of them was sitting at Bartlett's table.

Raquel said: "What is that woman doing here?"

Bartlett smiled at her uncertainly. "I couldn't get rid of her," he said.

Raquel turned on the prostitute and spoke vehemently in Hebrew. The woman who looked as if she might be knitting with a not-too-distant future in mind stood up quivering with affronted dignity. Raquel snapped at her once more and the woman moved to another table pulling a ball of wool behind her.

Raquel sat down and ordered a Gold Star beer.

Chapter 15

Raquel said: "Why don't you leave Israel, Thomas?"

Bartlett said: "Why?"

"Why? You ask me why? Because someone is trying to kill you—that's why."

They were walking up Allenby Street. It was nearly 1 P.M. and the exuberance in the streets was beginning to wane. At this time of day, Bartlett thought, you became more aware of the beggars and the vendors of cheap sunglasses and toy hammers that squeaked when you struck anyone with them. He liked to stop at the bookshops with their windows brazenly filled with books about Israel. The books were glossy and exotic and expensive.

Bartlett said: "When do you think I should leave?"

"Today," Raquel said.

"You seem very anxious to get rid of me."

"I don't want to see you hurt."

"I seem to have managed to take care of myself so far."

"You have managed?" She appealed to the lunchtime crowds. "He says he has managed. I ask you, what have you done?" Her voice softened a little. "Except of course to hold that terrorist." Her voice softened a little more. "You were very brave then, Thomas."

Because he didn't know what to reply Bartlett stopped outside a furnishing shop. He caught sight of his face in a mirror. His face was quite tanned, the effect marred by the skin beginning to peel off his nose.

Raquel said: "But really you have just been very lucky. It would be much better if you left."

"Not a chance," Bartlett said.

"You are a very foolish man."

"Perhaps. But you must be a very foolish girl consorting with me. Who knows—a gunman might have his sights on us right now."

Instinctively Raquel looked around. On one side of the road was the Great Synagogue, on the other Barclays Bank. She said: "I do not think they are trying to kill me."

"No," Bartlett said. "But they could be very bad shots. Perhaps that bullet in the Dead Sea was meant for me."

They went into a snack bar and ordered pizzas. Bartlett said: "It's difficult to believe that it's Sunday. I suppose that the answer is to be a Moslem working in the United States or British Embassies in Israel. That way you might get Friday, Saturday, and Sunday off."

"You are trying to evade the point," Raquel said.

"Which was?"

"Why don't you leave here today?"

"Because I came here to attend a geological conference. Because I intend to be present at that conference. Because I do not like cowardly people trying to intimidate me."

"Very well," she said. "Get yourself killed."

He chewed on his cheese and pastry and anchovies. "You seem very anxious to get rid of me. I rather thought you liked having me around."

"I do." She touched his arm. "You know I do. But do I want you dead?"

"Don't worry," he said. "No one's going to kill me."

"They've been having a damn good try. Are you sure it isn't your wife?"

He stopped chewing. "Why should it be?"

She smiled. "No reason. Just an Israeli joke."

110

"She's not particularly devoted to me. But I don't think she would go to that extreme."

"You don't talk about her much, do you? Most married men talk about their wives."

Bartlett's appetite froze. "Have you a lot of experience with married men?"

"No," she said. "Just you."

"Then how do you know that most married men talk about their wives?" He was appalled at the jealousy seeking expression.

"I have known married men. What girl has not known married men? They have told me about their wives. But that doesn't mean to say that I have had anything more to do with them."

"I suppose not. In any case I haven't any right to ask. I'm sorry." He ordered a large draught beer. "But, to answer your question, I don't talk about my wife because it doesn't seem right somehow. If things have gone wrong it's both our faults."

"Have you ever slept with another woman?"

Bartlett smiled into the big thick glass with the moisture already misting the outside. "That's more like the girl I met on the plane."

"I told you Israeli girls are nosey."

"You gave me fair warning."

"But still you have not answered my question. You have a very good knack of evading questions you don't want to answer, Mr Bartlett. Have you slept with another woman since you got married to this wife of yours?"

"Very nosey and very personal. Honestly, the Arabs don't stand a chance."

"Have you, Thomas?"

"No," he said. He vaguely felt that the admission was a criticism of his character.

"I didn't think so."

"Was it so obvious, then?" He remembered some of Helen's remarks.

111

"No it was not." She leaned across the table. "You are a beautiful lover."

He looked around the snack bar and said: "I wish you'd keep your voice down a bit."

"And I wish you'd stop acting the part of a stage Englishman." She lowered her voice. "Can we make love again tonight, Thomas?"

"Not if I leave the country," he said.

"I would rather that you stay alive and that we do not make love tonight." She sipped her Coke. "I could always come to London and see you there. Or perhaps we could meet somewhere else. Cyprus, perhaps. A lot of people fly to Cyprus from here for holidays." Her enthusiasm gained momentum. "Why not Cyprus, Thomas? Why don't you catch a plane to Cyprus and I will join you there? Kyrenia is a beautiful place. We could swim and sunbathe there and make love at night."

"What about the daytime?"

"In the daytime, too. You would like it there. And there is a lot that would interest you as a geologist, I promise you."

"I know," Bartlett said. "I've been there."

"Then will you go?"

He shook his head. "I'm afraid not, Raquel. It would seem like cowardice. I don't know what on earth this is all about but I intend to find out."

"Please," she said.

"No," he said.

"Then you cannot love me."

"Don't be childish." He paid the bill. "You know I've got to stay here. You wouldn't really respect me if I left you now. Would an Israeli leave in these circumstances?"

She sighed. "Perhaps not."

"Would your fiancé have left?"

"How did you know about my fiancé?"

"I guessed. No girl as beautiful as you can live in a virile country like this without having a fiancé."

"He's dead," Raquel said.

"I guessed as much."

"It was over a year ago. The terrorists threw a grenade in Gaza and a splinter struck him." She stood up to leave. "You don't despise me now because I have made love so soon after his death?"

Bartlett wished again that she would keep her voice down. "A year is a long time," he said. "Especially in this part of the world. No, I do not despise you." He wanted to add that he loved her; but he wasn't sure that he did.

"It just happened," she said.

"I know," he said. "Let's move on—everyone seems rather interested in our conversation here."

"Very well," she said. "In any case we must be getting back to Jerusalem."

"There's something I'd like to do first."

"What is that?"

"I'd like to go on the beach," Bartlett said.

"You want to go on the beach?" She peered at his face. "I tell you it would not be wise. Already your nose is peeling."

"It will be all right. First we must buy a pair of trunks and perhaps go back to your apartment. You have some tanning lotion?"

She nodded. "But I do not see why you should want to go on the beach. I do not think it would be good for you."

"I might be a bit pale," Bartlett said. "But I think I can stand a bit of sunshine."

At the apartment Bartlett liberally applied cream to his face. On the beach he kept his shirt on and put more cream on his arms and legs. Around him the bodies were very brown —the men lithe, the girls bouncy.

Raquel was wearing a white one-piece which unwove itself into net around her waist. Her belly was flat and her small breasts firm. Bartlett anticipated their return to the hotel in Jerusalem with pleasure.

"There don't appear to be many people swimming," he said. "They're all patting those damn balls around instead."

"Israel is not a nation of swimmers," Raquel said. "Too

many of its people came from places where there were no opportunities to swim."

They were at the end of a strip of sand that stretched out to sea from the base of one of the new American hotels to a breakwater where drenched anglers stood among plumes of spray. In front of them an old woman with wrinkled brown skin was doing her exercises; two pale men with wobbling stomachs walking briskly up and down the water's edge.

"Tourists," Raquel said.

"Is everyone white and out-of-condition a tourist?"

"Usually," she said. She looked at his pale legs. "I cannot make out what we are doing here. It does not seem right somehow."

Bartlett grinned at her. "A spot of mild sadism, British style."

"What are you talking about, Thomas?"

"I noticed Yosevitz following us earlier. If ever there was a man who will fry up in the sun it's him."

When they got back to Bartlett's room in the hotel at Jerusalem the detective whom Bartlett had consulted was waiting there.

"Shalom," he said. "Is this the young lady you were telling me about?"

Bartlett said: "This is Miss Rabinovitz."

"I should like to have a few private words with you, Mr Bartlett."

Raquel said: "I'll come back in half an hour." She spoke emphatically implying that she saw no reason why she should not be in Bartlett's room.

After she had gone the detective, who looked like a middle-aged Ben-Gurion, said: "I see what you mean, Mr Bartlett."

"You do?"

"About Miss Rabinovitz. A man could become jealous over her."

"Someone is pretty annoyed about something."

"I know, Mr Bartlett. I must apologise about my previous

attitude. In fact we are getting quite worried about you. How much longer are you staying in this country?"

"I'm not sure. Longer than I expected. I have just heard that the conference will not now open until Wednesday."

"I really think it would be very wise of you to leave before then. Is this conference so important to you?"

"Yes it is," Bartlett said. "That's funny—you're the second person who has suggested that I should leave as soon as possible."

"Really. May I ask who the first was?"

"I don't think it would help you," Bartlett said. "Anyway, why do you want me to leave so suddenly? The other day you weren't very concerned about my welfare. Is it perhaps the security of Israel that concerns you more than my future on this earth?"

The detective sat on a chair in front of the dressing-table mirror so that Bartlett found he was looking at both his face and the back of his head. The detective said: "During your short stay in Israel there has been one attempt on your life, one incident in which an American was shot dead and an unsuccessful bid by El Fatah terrorists to kidnap you."

"You make it sound like an indictment," Bartlett said.

"Not an indictment, Mr Bartlett, a catalogue. We do not want that catalogue to get any longer."

"You," Bartlett said irritably, "are not the only one."

"Then would it not be easier for everyone concerned if you left as soon as possible?"

"It might well be easier," Bartlett said. "But I am the most interested party and I have no intention of leaving."

"It would not be difficult for me to make sure that you leave," the detective said. He paused. "In fact, Mr Bartlett, we could probably put you on an aircraft today."

"Deportation? On what grounds?" Bartlett's anger was mounting. "Look Mr . . ."

"Levinsky."

"Look, Mr Levinsky. I have endured a lot since I came to your country. None of it the fault of the Israelis—as far as I know. In fact I am most impressed with your countrymen. But I do not intend to be expelled merely because another attempt on my life could be an embarrassment to you."

Levinsky rumpled his thick greying hair. "I did not expect quite such spirit," he said. "You know, of course, that we do not have to give any reason for a deportation order."

"Don't worry," Bartlett said. "I would give plenty of reasons when I landed at London Airport."

Levinsky smiled. "You are as aggressive as an Israeli fighting man."

"No," Bartlett said. "Just obstinate. Your job is to protect me not to give me my marching orders."

Levinsky sighed. "You are absolutely right, of course, Mr Bartlett, but I'm afraid . . ."

He was interrupted by a knock on the door. A porter said: "Excuse me, sir, there is a telephone call downstairs for Mr Levinsky."

Bartlett said: "Can't he take it here?"

The porter said: "The caller particularly asked that Mr Levinsky take the call downstairs."

While Levinksy was gone Bartlett sat on the edge of the bed and contemplated developments. In fact he was by no means convinced that there was no Israeli complicity in the violent events of the past few days. He suspected that if he was forced to leave the country someone would be watching him when he picked up the hidden documents.

But why were the contents so important? The answer did not come to Bartlett with startling impact. He realised that he had slowly been approaching the answer for some time with a geologist's caution, and suspicion of facile explanation. But even so it was only half the answer.

Levinksy looked puzzled when he returned.

"Well?" Bartlett said.

"It was just a routine call."

"Couldn't you have taken it up here?"

"You have a very suspicious nature, Mr Bartlett."

116

"All geologists are the same."

"I suppose so. I didn't realise it before."

"Well, are you going to deport me?"

"That's a very strong word, Mr Bartlett."

"I'm not concerned with any euphemism that you choose to use. Are you going to deport me?"

Levinsky stared at himself in the mirror. "I think perhaps it will not be necessary. I did not realise that you were quite so determined to stay. I was merely suggesting that you leave for your own good."

The new awareness that had joined Bartlett's sensibilities since his arrival in Israel reasserted itself. "You were not *suggesting*," he said. "Could your change in attitude have anything to do with that phone call you just received?"

Levinsky turned away from the mirror. "Mr Bartlett," he said, "you are probably an excellent geologist. You would also have made an excellent detective."

He walked to the door and hesitated there. He still looked puzzled and unsure of himself. It was not, Bartlett knew, a characteristic attitude. He started to speak, then shook his head and walked out into the corridor.

They lay beneath a sheet, tranquil and satisfied after the act of love. Bartlett smoked a cigarette with one hand and held her hand with the other. The room was drowsy with dusk; outside the first stars were establishing themselves in the advancing darkness.

"What are you thinking?" she said.

Helen always wanted to know what he was thinking, but with exasperation rather than unbridled curiosity. He had, in fact, been marvelling at his appetite for love. Helen had always derided his waning interest—and made it wane even more.

"I was just thinking about the sort of visit I envisaged before I set out from London," he said. "A dullish conference enlivened by a few tourist attractions."

"And now you've got me," she said. "I'm your tourist attraction."

117

"Yes," he said. "I think I would forego Masada for you."

The last luminosity of day was fading. Bartlett stubbed out his cigarette and ran his hand over the sheet, lingering at the small hillocks of her breasts. He was moved with a sense of sharing—their dusk, their stars emerging. And surprised to find himself lying naked beside a beautiful Jewish girl overlooking the foundation stones of religion.

"Would you like a drink?" he said.

"I do not mind."

He made a robe out of a towel and poured the remains of the whisky he had bought in the aircraft into two tumblers. He lingered at the window and looked at Jerusalem. At the divided city tenuously unified. Lights burned in the Bible blackness and the outlines of domes, spires, and minarets were precise against the last green gleam of day. Never had politics and the contrived enmities of Mankind seemed quite so futile.

She said: "Could I have my drink, please." He handed it to her. "You look very noble in profile," she said. "What were you thinking about then?"

"I wish I could devise some way by which my thoughts were transferred to you without the effort of speaking."

"Again you are evasive. What were you thinking about? Was it about your wife?"

"No. Just a few hackneyed observations about Jerusalem!" He drew the curtains and put on the bed lamp. He slipped under the sheet, removed the towel and moved close to her.

"Thomas."

"Yes?"

"When are you going back to England?"

"After the conference, I suppose." He had been purposely diverting all conversation from the subject.

"Will we ever see each other again after that?"

"Of course we will." As always he found her directness disconcerting.

"You do not sound very convincing. What would you do if I came to London?"

"See you, of course." He thought of Helen and of the deceit that would be involved. But was deceit necessary? After all she had been betraying him for a long time.

"And would you show me England just as I've shown you Israel?"

"Of course I would."

She stroked his chest. "Dear Thomas—I do not believe you. Why do you not stay here? A little longer anyway. Then perhaps you would like our country so much that you would want to stay and help my people. You could do a lot for us Israelis with your geology."

He put his hand on her breast. "If people would stop trying to kill me and steal my property I might be a little more enthusiastic."

"You take it all so calmly," she said.

"It's easier now," he said.

"Easier? You say it is easier? I ask you—how can it be easier?"

Bartlett raised himself on one elbow so that he could see her face. "Because I think I understand a little what it's all about."

He watched the expression on her face very carefully. She frowned and put one hand to her lips. "You understand what it's all about?"

"A little, I think."

She put down her tumbler of whisky on the bedside table. "Well, tell me, Thomas. What is it all about?"

"I'll tell you later," he said. "When I'm sure."

"You don't trust me."

"I do. I just want to be sure." He bent and kissed her and thought how warm and dry her lips were. At first there was no response; then her lips parted slightly. And Bartlett found to his astonishment that he was ready to make love to her again.

119

As he tried to shave his red and shiny jowels in his hotel bedroom, Matthew Yosevitz decided to kill Ralston.

The killing, he thought, might appease his thwarted professional instincts and settle the general confusion of his thoughts.

So far the whole mission had gone disastrously wrong. He ascribed the failures to several factors—the inefficiency of his Arab collaborators, his confused loyalties, the extraordinary capability for survival exhibited by the Englishman, and American interference. At least he could terminate the latter by dispatching Ralston in the wake of Everett.

It would have to be shooting. Yosevitz had been trained to assassinate by many methods. But none gave him the same professional satisfaction as execution with a gun. One bullet, neat, clean, and permanent.

He washed the shaving soap from his burning cheeks and daubed them with calamine. But the effect was clownish. He washed the calamine off the first degree burns and cursed Bartlett.

He picked up his pistol from beneath the towel lying across the chair beside the bed. With the silencer fitted it looked completely professional.

Then he began to dress, cringing his burning face through his vest and cheap nylon shirt. As he laced up his bruised shoes he acknowledged another important reason for his decision to kill Ralston: it would not be a directly anti-Jewish act that would further disturb his conscience.

In the past couple of days the rift between his loyalties had widened. All around him he sensed the urgency and determination of the Jews to survive in their new land. His land. No, he was a Communist dedicated to the extermination of capitalism; dedicated to the establishment of equality throughout the world. But there was a lot of equality in Israel . . .

A couple of Mirage jets whistled over the hotel. Probably returning from a rocket-attack on Jordanian positions across the river. A torch of pride four thousand years old briefly flared in Yosevitz's soul. It was immediately extinguished by reality: his wife and two children were in Warsaw and it was them and the millions like them for whom he was working.

So, as he combed his thin hair away from his burned forehead, he tried to plan the killing of Ralston with something of his old singlemindedness. Ralston was an American agent and therefore his death could only be advantageous to the Communist cause; Ralston was not apparently working with the Israelis, therefore Judaism would not suffer directly. It was very satisfactory.

Yosevitz picked up the phone and ordered some coffee and hard-boiled eggs.

According to his local contacts Bartlett was staying in the hotel until 11 A.M. and Ralston was going into the Old City—possibly to meet someone from the United States Embassy. The shooting would have to be in the Old City. At close range among the crowds thronging the alleys. Hardly a sound from the good professional gun, the body propped up momentarily by the crowds, the assassin lost in the throng.

This time he would not seek the co-operation of any Arab. Not after Hamid's efforts at snatching an empty briefcase and the fiasco at El Hamma.

Yosevitz wondered where Bartlett had hidden the contents of the briefcase. Probably, with obscure British humour, at some religious monument. At the Citadel perhaps, or even the El Aqsa Mosque. In any case he would have to be captured and probably killed because he knew what had been in the case.

Yosevitz strapped on his holster. Unfortunately that meant keeping his jacket on. He was aware that the combination of a jacket and flaming face would make him doubly incongruous. But at least he would not be following Bartlett of whose face and figure he was heartily sick.

He let himself out of his room and walked down the corridor. Even when there was no cause his sharp-toed shoes moved delicately and stealthily.

Ralston entered the Old City by St Stephen's Gate. He walked past the St Anne Monastery towards the Via Dolorosa. Yosevitz followed at a distance of about a hundred yards hoping that the snap-brimmed plastic hat and the steel-rimmed French sunglasses were sufficient disguise.

Ralston walked quickly despite the gathering heat. His sense of purpose convinced Yosevitz that he was on his way to meet a contact. It was, he thought, a welcome change to be stalking a fellow professional—at least he wouldn't suddenly go sunbathing. Yosevitz's hand strayed to his glowing cheeks; sweat trickled down his back and chest under his nylon shirt.

Ralston stopped near the Ecce Homo Arch and went inside a dark coffee shop. Yosevitz stopped, leaned against a wall and read his guide book. *The Ecce Homo Arch recalls the words of Pilate's address to Jesus, "Behold the Man."* Yosevitz glanced down the street: there was no sign of Ralston. *The Ecce Homo was part of the triple triumphal arch erected by Roman Emperor Hadrian in the second century . . .* Yosevitz decided to see what was happening in the coffee shop. He walked quickly past glancing to one side behind his green plastic lenses. Ralston was sitting by himself at a table covered with oilcloth. He was drinking coffee and smoking a cigarette while an Arab boy brushed his shoes.

Yosevitz walked on fifty yards and consulted his map. In

the Old City there was a Moslem quarter, a Christian quarter, an Armenian quarter, and a Jewish quarter. So much belief. Yosevitz remembered the beautiful old churches of Russia and the candles burning steadfastly in their eternal dusk while Soviet youth jeered outside.

He slipped his hand inside his jacket. He was going to kill an American agent. A representative of a power that threatened the peace of the world. It was no time to brood on faith.

A small boy in a black suit with a white shirt buttoned at the collar but no tie prodded a friend in the ribs and pointed at Yosevitz. They both had short hair with ringlets trained down their cheeks. Ahead of them lay a lifetime of faith. Yosevitz thought of his own son, eight years old and already knowledgeable about Communism. Just as he had been.

One of the boys spoke in Hebrew. He said: "Hasn't that man got a red face."

His friend nodded and giggled.

Yosevitz stared at them menacingly through his big green spectacles and they ran away down the Via Dolorosa. Ralston came out of the cafe and stood outside absorbing the sunshine. Yosevitz shrank back into a shop selling camel saddles and brass coffeepots.

An Arab approached him and said eagerly: "What would you like to buy, sir. Make me happy and buy one of these saddles for your fine horse."

Yosevitz said: "Shut up and go away."

He spoke with such distilled vehemence that the Arab backed away across the shop, pain and astonishment on his bargain-price face.

Ralston walked past, still tasting the sunshine. Yosevitz gave him half a minute and then fell into place behind him. Ralston turned left and headed down the Suq Khan Ez-zeit in the direction of the Jewish quarter.

For the killing the circumstances had to be exactly right. A dense, noisy crowd and an escape route.

Ralston turned left along Bab El-Silsileh Road and crossed

123

it as if he were heading for the ruined synagogues. Instead he continued along the road towards the Western Wall. Twice he paused and looked behind him. Yosevitz shrank into doorways like a sea anemone that has been touched.

The crowds were packed thickly in front of the wall. Yosevitz fingered his gun; it was warm and damp. He waited patiently while Ralston stood gazing at the great blocks of sand-coloured stone. Pilgrims looked curiously at Yosevitz's bright face. He opened his guide book and read about the wall: *Often called the Wailing Wall, it is the last remnant of western wall bounding outer court of Herod's magnificent Temple. Lowest tiers date from Solomon's First Temple. Age-old place of Jewish lamentation and prayer for its restoration.*

As he waited to kill Ralston the idea began to form in Yosevitz's mind that he, too, should offer a prayer at the wall. At first it presented itself whimsically. But Yosevitz was not one for whimsy: the notion hardened. Why not? It could do no harm. Despite his upbringing and environment he was, after all, a Jew. And the Jews had fought bravely to regain the wall. Yosevitz decided that a prayer from a pilgrim from Moscow could not harm the cause of Communism.

But then his training asserted itself. What if someone was keeping observation on him? In his youth there had always been someone watching or listening. It was part of the system. Was it not conceivable that the system was operating now? He looked round him. But you could never tell—he knew that.

He watched an Orthodox Jew in a wide-brimmed black hat push through the crowd to the wall; he placed his hands on a ledge and bowed his head. Again the call came to Yosevitz, knifing through twenty years of ideological teaching.

In front of him Ralston spoke to a tall, balding man in light grey trousers and short-sleeved tropical-weight shirt. The embassy contact, perhaps. The newcomer was undoubtedly American—freckled and muscular and dependable. He carried the inevitable camera and a pack of cigarettes in the breast pocket of his shirt.

Ralston and his contact lit cigarettes. Yosevitz noted that it was Ralston who leaned forward to accept a light and narrowed his eyes to see if a message was being passed; but he saw nothing except their cupped hands. They nodded, smiled, spoke briefly, and parted.

Ralston dropped his cigarette and squashed it with his heel. Yosevitz tensed himself. He was no longer aware of the sun toasting his red cheeks. Ralston walked towards the wall. The Orthodox Jew whom Yosevitz had been watching was still praying; the sound of lamentation filled the air.

Ralston stopped at the stall beside the enclosure directly in front of the wall. He glanced round and Yosevitz stared at his guide book through his green plastic lenses. Ralston took a cardboard hat from the stall and edged through the crowd to the wall.

Yosevitz, who had intended to follow, stopped. The gun felt hard against his ribs. He knew now he couldn't use it. It was the hat that had done it. The stupid, idiotic cardboard hat on Ralston's head. He didn't quite know why. But you did not shoot a man in a cardboard hat.

Ralston stayed at the wall for a minute. Then returned to the stall and handed back his hat.

After Ralston had disappeared Yosevitz walked up to the stall, then realised that he was already wearing a hat, a plastic hat. He approached the wall, cheeks burning, loyalties reeling. If only Ralston hadn't put on the cardboard hat.

Chapter 17

It was Saturday evening. The air smelled of grass recently cut; a couple of bats dipped and swooped in the uncertain light.

Helen Bartlett shut the French windows and switched on the television. But she couldn't concentrate. She went into the lounge, mixed herself a Martini cocktail and reviewed the situation with some bitterness: her husband was in Israel, her lover was unobtainable—he had been for the past few days—and her employment at the American Embassy had been terminated.

Cocktail in hand she continued her restless patrol of the house and stopped in her husband's study. His desk was as untidy as ever—sheafs of papers anchored with stones shaped like flat snails. The appendages of his profession had always annoyed her because she couldn't understand them.

But why had they sacked her? There had never been any complaints about her work. Could it be her association with Ahmed? She didn't see why: she hadn't communicated any embassy secrets. In fact the only information she had imparted had been connected with Tom's visit to Israel.

She swallowed her Martini and went into the lounge to mix another. Through the door the television filled the adjoining room with blue and grey animation. She listened vaguely to the newcaster's voice. Nasser had made a speech in which he said the Arabs would fight their way to victory regardless of bloodshed or suffering. A commentator then quenched some of the fire by explaining that the speech was probably made to appease extreme Arab elements challenging the recognised leadership.

But to Helen Bartlett, the speech had an ominous and personal message. She thought of Ahmed, his immovable cap of hair, his unflagging virility. Could she in some way have betrayed her husband by discussing his business with an Arab? It didn't really seem possible. But the dusk, the loneliness, Nasser's speech, and the Martinis awakened instincts of worry and affection.

She poured herself another Martini and returned to the study to consult Tom's itinerary. He should now be at the Intercontinental in Jerusalem. Suddenly she wished she was there with him. She picked up the phone, asked for the international exchange and put through a call to Jerusalem.

Then she sat down, tinkled the ice in her glass and regretted the errors of her marriage. If only Tom had been more assertive, more interested in her than he had been in the strata of the earth. But every man had a right to be absorbed with his job. Helen Bartlett felt so sad that she returned to the lounge and poured herself the last of the cocktail from the shaker.

In the past she had accused Tom of infidelity. The accusation now seemed ludicrous. It was merely that, with his disordered ways, he appeared to many women to be fair game. The bitches. She had been condemning Tom when she should have been condemning the women.

The call came within five minutes. She heard a woman's voice saying, "Jerusalem on the line." There was a confusion of voices; then, although the call was person-to-person, another woman's voice announced the name of the hotel.

Helen said: "Is Mr Bartlett there, please?"

The woman's voice which had a slight American accent said: "Do you mean Mr Bartlett of the Geological Conference?"

"Yes," Helen said. "That's the Mr Bartlett I mean."

"I don't think he's here right now. I believe he stayed the night in Tel Aviv."

Then another woman cut in. "Is that Miss Rabinovitz on the line for Mr Bartlett?" She sounded like another hotel switchboard operator.

The first woman said: "Could you get off the line please —I am talking to London."

Helen Bartlett said: "Who was that? Who is Miss Rabinovitz?"

"I don't know, I'm sure. I'm sorry about the interruption. Can I take a message for you?"

Helen said: "Do you have a number for Mr Bartlett in Tel Aviv?"

"No, I'm sorry. But if I can leave a message . . ."

Helen said: "No, don't worry." She replaced the receiver.

Miss Rabinovitz. Who the hell was Miss Rabinovitz?

She picked up the phone again and called Ahmed. Instead of Ahmed she got an answering service. She hung up again.

She went into the lounge and made herself one more Martini, small and strong, and sat in front of the television. The news was over and there was a feature about the Sinai on the screen. But instead of camels and Bedouins it seemed to Helen that the desert was populated by plump-breasted Israeli girl soldiers. She leaned forward and switched over to the other channel.

Chapter 18

Bartlett looked at his watch. It was 10:30 A.M.—half an hour before Raquel was due to pick him up. They were going into the Sinai for two days following the further postponement of the conference. Bartlett blessed the bacillus that had attacked his fellow geologists.

He decided with some trepidation to have the showdown with her when they were four hours out of Jerusalem. He set the alarm on the gimmicky wrist watch for 3 P.M.

His feelings about guessing Raquel's true occupation were confused. He was delighted with his perspicacity but sad that she had not been able to trust him.

He picked up the phone and ordered a Gold Star. The identification of Raquel's role in recent events had not been particularly astute. A professional agent would have classified her on the aircraft; but, he thought, it was not bad for a man whose job was classifying rocks.

It had been a process of elimination. The Arabs wanted the contents of the briefcase. So did the Russians—through the agency of the Polish Jew Yosevitz. Everett had been an American agent and there were no prizes for guessing the identity of his successor—although Ralston looked so much like a policeman that you tended to eliminate him. That left one interested party unaccounted for. But Bartlett respected Israeli efficiency too much to believe that they were not in the game. It had to be Raquel.

129

He paid for the beer and sipped it standing at his bedroom window gazing over Jerusalem.

What was still puzzling was the motive for pursuit and attempted murder. He had reread the paper he proposed to deliver to the conference. It seemed harmless enough. Which meant it had to be the maps. God knows why. But he was quite prepared to play the game.

His new determination surprised him. It had only happened once before when, with the world's geological opinion against him, he had determined to prove a principle relating to the formation of the Rockies. He had been right.

Bartlett finished the ice-cold beer and glanced at his watch again. It was 10:40.

The knock on the door was sharp, almost aggressive.

Bartlett said: "Okay, I'm coming."

But when he opened the door he found Ralston, not Raquel, waiting outside.

Ralston said: "I guess it's about time we put our cards on the table, Mr Bartlett."

Bartlett said: "I think it's about time you put your cards on the table, Mr Ralston."

Ralston sat on the chair in front of the dressing table. All his inquisitors sat there, Bartlett thought. In the mirror he could see Ralston's powerful neck with the skin just beginning to crease.

Ralston nodded. "I figured that even you wouldn't be convinced that El Hamma was a coincidence."

"I resent the phrase 'even you,'" Bartlett said.

Ralston said: "I'm sorry. We don't seem to be getting off to a great start, do we."

Bartlett said nothing.

Ralston lit a cigarette with his big lighter. "You'll have to excuse me," he said. "I'm just recovering from an unnerving experience. I had some guy with a gun stalking me in the Old City. I thought he might take a shot at me but he chickened out at the last moment. We had someone right

130

behind him so I guess I would have lived whatever happened. But I still can't figure out why he lost his nerve—he isn't the type."

"Who, Yosevitz?"

The surprise on Ralston's face pleased Bartlett. "You know about him?"

"I know he tried to kill me. I suspect he *did* kill your predecessor. I also suspect that he's got a very red face today."

Again Ralston looked surprised. "He has as a matter of fact. How the hell did you know that?"

"He was following me yesterday and I led him on to the beach. I rather thought he wasn't the tanning type."

Ralston grinned. "Mr Bartlett," he said, "you continue to amaze me. So you were wise to me and you were wise to Yosevitz. The Arabs have tried to snatch your briefcase and kidnap you. That leaves the Israelis. Are you wise to the Israelis, Mr Bartlett?"

Bartlett nodded. "You don't have to be Hercule Poirot to work that one out."

"The girl?"

"Of course," Bartlett said.

"And yet you still encourage her?"

"Wouldn't you?"

Ralston considered the question for a moment. "Yes, I guess I would," he said.

"And she will be here in five minutes."

"In that case," Ralston said, "we'd better get down to business. We have a lot to discuss, Mr Bartlett."

"You have a lot to explain," Bartlett said.

"You have in your possession some very important maps. It's those maps that everyone is after."

"I rather gathered that," Bartlett said. "Would it not have been easier if someone had asked me for them?"

"Everett tried to but you wouldn't give him a chance."

"I suppose so." Bartlett glanced at his watch. Raquel was due in three minutes. "But if people want these maps why do they try to shoot me and kidnap me?"

"That's quite simple," Ralston said. "On the first occasion Yosevitz saw you out walking without your briefcase. He reckoned it would be easy enough to get the case from your hotel. He also reckoned with the characteristic thoroughness of the KGB that as you would know what was on those maps so it would be necessary to kill you."

"And the kidnapping at El Hamma?"

"I can only guess at that. But I figure the Arabs were insisting on taking some active part in the plan, because they don't take too kindly to being under the thumb of the Soviets. No one loves their benefactor, you know."

"Then why didn't they just try and kill me?"

"Because by this time you had been cute enough to hide the maps. If I know anything about Arab methods I reckon they would have tortured you until you revealed the hiding place. I think you would agree that you owe me something, Mr Bartlett. Your life, for instance."

"I've already thanked you."

"You could be a little more generous."

"You mean I could tell you where I've hidden the maps?"

"Right." Ralston smiled candidly at the simplicity of it all.

"Can you give me one good reason why I should tell you?"

"Unless you're a Communist or an Arab sympathiser I shouldn't have thought that was necessary."

"You forget, Mr Ralston, that I don't know why you want those maps."

"I'll be frank with you Mr Bartlett . . ."

Bartlett's new awareness stirred. It said: That means that Ralston will be everything but frank.

Ralston weighed the big lighter in his hand and contemplated his large shoes. "The fact of the matter is that those maps can play a vital part in negotiating peace in the Middle East. I feel sure that you wouldn't want to stand in the way of peace."

"I'll be frank with you, Mr Ralston . . ." Bartlett smiled. "I do not like people trying to interfere with my life. In particular I do not like them trying to rob and kill me. In

132

particular the latter. Certainly I would not wish to do anything that would jeopardize peace. But just as certainly I want to know what this is all about. I want to know just how those maps can affect the future of the Middle East. I know those maps and frankly I can't see it."

Ralston sighed. "It's very difficult to explain. Can't you just trust me? I promise you that it's in the interest of the West and the fewer people who know the better."

Bartlett examined Ralston's honest-looking face and said: "No, I can't."

Ralston stood up and gazed across Jerusalem. "You're making things very difficult. Especially when there's so little time."

"Did you forge that note in Tel Aviv authorising the hotel porter to hand my briefcase over to you?"

Ralston sighed, more heavily this time. "I'm afraid so. I need those maps."

"I don't like people forging my signature," Bartlett said. "Please continue with your explanation."

Ralston said: "Sooner or later Israel is going to have to make a concession and give up some territory. It could just be that such a concession would appease the Arabs despite all the sabre-rattling from Nasser. Whoever has your maps will be in a stronger bargaining position than their opponents."

"Why?"

"I don't really want to go into that too deeply," Ralston said.

"That I believe," Bartlett said. He looked at his watch again. "You've got one minute in which to convince me. And I must warn you that I don't much care for the word bargaining. Tell me this, Mr Ralston, if these maps are so vital to negotiated peace why don't we just give them to the Israelis?"

"If you must know," Ralston said, "we reckon this whole thing should be handled at four-power level."

"Why?"

"Jesus," Ralston said, "for a bumbly geologist you sure do ask the darnedest questions."

"Geologists aren't all bumbly," Bartlett said.

"Okay, okay. Anyway we think the whole thing should be hammered out at four-power level. It is, after all, the world's problem. It *is* world peace that's threatened. It shouldn't be left to the Israelis and the Arabs."

Bartlett's new awareness sharpened into intuition. "I have a strange feeling that your heart isn't in that last remark."

Ralston mimed exasperation. "The earth's stratum doesn't stand much of a chance with a guy like you around," he said. "Okay, maybe I'm not a politician either. All I know is that the President of the United States thinks that this should be hammered out at the highest level there is."

A few of the words that he had overheard on the crossed wire came back to Bartlett. Something about prestige. He said: "I wish for once you'd be absolutely honest with me. I have the maps, remember."

"In what way am I not being honest?"

"It's not just a question of believing that discussion at four-power level is the best way of ensuring peace, is it? American prestige is at stake, is it not, Mr Ralston?"

"In a way, I guess." Ralston sat down again and exhibited the back of his neck to Bartlett in the mirror: it seemed to have acquired another crease since they started talking. Ralston said: "Put it like this, Mr Bartlett. The whole motive behind this operation is peace. Please take my word for that. I wouldn't be involved if it wasn't. Sure, American prestige is involved, too. Why not? We want peace but we don't surely want the Soviets to take all the credit for it, do we?"

"I don't see that it matters who takes the credit as long as you stop these people killing each other."

Ralston spoke with elaborate patience. "That's what we aim to do. America wants to stop the killing. But we want it done cleanly and fairly—not on Communist terms. Is there anything wrong with that?"

Bartlett shook his head. "There's nothing wrong with that."

134

"Then why are you holding back for God's sake?"

"For the simple reason that until now I had no idea what you were all after."

"But you heard the President talking to the Ambassador. You must have known what it was all about."

Bartlett decided not to tell Ralston that he had been overcome by an attack of hay fever. He didn't want to appear too "bumbly" to this tough, efficient American. He said: "I couldn't make out what it was all about. For that matter I'm still not sure. You'll have to explain a little better. Mr. Ralston. You've only got about thirty seconds. But you could be lucky—she could be late."

"I thought I had explained."

"You still haven't explained to me the importance of these maps."

"I don't think I want to do that, Mr Bartlett. If you don't realise their importance then I reckon it would be better for you not to understand. Now, please, tell me where you've hidden them."

Bartlett shook his head. "It's not on, I'm afraid. Not on these terms, anyway. If I can help the cause of peace then I will do everything in my power to do so. But you need to be a little more explicit than that."

Ralston looked at the big deep-sea diving watch on his wrist. "Are you going to tell me where those maps are?"

"Not unless you can explain a little better. I must know why you need them. That's fair enough, isn't it? For all I know I might be playing into the hands of big business. And in any case I want to be in a position to make up my own mind. I'm getting very tired of being pushed around."

"You won't accept that it's better for the United States of America to have those maps than the Arabs or the Russians?"

"Or the Israelis?"

"I'm sorry about this," Ralston said. "I think you're a good guy. But we just haven't the time." He took a .45 Colt from inside his jacket. "But it's like this, Mr Bartlett. At the moment no one knows where you've hidden those maps. And the only

135

person who knows what's in them is yourself. If you won't tell me where they are then I shall have no alternative but to shoot you."

Bartlett looked at the pistol. A police-issue, he thought. It had to be. He smiled because he wasn't frightened.

Ralston said: "This sure as hell isn't a smiling matter."

"I've learned quite a bit in the past few days," Bartlett said. "I know that you wouldn't shoot me. Not here anyway. There'd be too much of a stink and in any case you'd get yourself arrested."

Ralston's finger stroked the trigger. "I'm afraid I can't go along with you on that one. I rescued you, remember? I figure that most people—Miss Rabinovitz included—would believe that Yosevitz killed you."

"With a .45 Colt?"

Ralston said: "You amaze me. You really do. I thought I'd be dealing with the original absent-minded professor. Now you turn out to be a little old authority on ballistics."

"Not really," Bartlett said. "But it stands to reason that a Polish Jew representing the Russians would hardly be shooting people with an American police-issue pistol. No, Mr Ralston, I don't think you would kill me here with that gun." He stood up. "In fact I don't think you want to shoot me anyway."

Ralston stuffed the gun away. "No, I guess you're right. There's no harm in trying to threaten you. I should have known better now I come to think of it. You didn't improve that Arab's vocal chords with the neck-lock you put on him."

"Shouldn't you slug me or something?"

Ralston shook his head. "No, no slugging. Where are those goddamn maps?"

"I'll tell you what I'll do," Bartlett said. "I promise that I won't help the Arabs or the Russians."

"And the Israelis?"

"And the Israelis. I want to do this thing on my own. Believe it or not but I have a few ideas myself. In fact I think I can handle it better than you."

"Please leave it to the professionals, Mr Bartlett."

"From what I've seen of the professionals I think I can do a better job."

"You do me an injustice."

"All right, present company excepted. But I'm still going to handle it myself. For a couple of days at least."

"This wouldn't have anything to do with the fact that you're going into the Sinai with Miss Rabinovitz?"

"How did you know?"

"I'm a professional, Mr Bartlett. I have contacts in this City. So does Yosevitz. He's a professional too. You can bet your bottom lira that he knows where you're going too. You have, I believe, ordered a jeep."

"Raquel has."

"An Israeli agent, Mr Bartlett. You know that as well as I do. She must have made her play by now. Have you told her anything about those maps?"

"She's asked one or two questions. I haven't given her the answers."

"Do you promise that you won't? She is a very attractive girl. In the desert, under the stars—can you be so goddamn sure that you won't tell her anything?"

"I can be sure."

"Okay then. I'm going to trust you. I reckon maybe I'm nuts or something. But anyway I'll trust you. If you give that information to anyone it will be to me. Right?"

"I promised you that I wouldn't help anyone else."

"Okay," Ralston said. "I'll go along with that."

"You can't really do anything else," Bartlett said.

They sat watching each other waiting for the knock on the door. It came within a few seconds. Bartlett said: "Who's that?"

She said: "It's me. Raquel. Who else did you expect."

"You never know," Bartlett said.

He opened the door and she came in. He observed her controlled surprise when she saw Ralston.

"Good morning," Ralston said. "I was just leaving."

"Good morning," she said.

Ralston turned to Bartlett and said: "I'll keep you to that, Mr Bartlett. Don't forget."

"I won't," Bartlett said.

Ralston walked out of the room with his measured tread.

Bartlett looked speculatively at Raquel. He hoped that she would tell him the truth about herself before he had to confront her with his knowledge. She had exactly four hours in which to do so.

At last, he thought, he had the advantage over them all. Because, although he had pleaded ignorance to Ralston, he now knew why everyone wanted the maps—or one of them. It should have been obvious to him before. But then he had certain information of which they knew nothing.

*

Chapter 19

They struck southwest towards Gaza.

Bartlett said: "You handle a jeep very well."

"I learned when I was a soldier," she said.

"When you were a policewoman, you mean. Do you always get your jeep from the same place?"

"Always." She frowned. "Why do you ask?"

"I suggest you try somewhere else in future."

"What are you talking about, Thomas? Today you talk in riddles." She swung out and overtook three half-tracks, waving at the crews. "And what was Mr Ralston doing in your room?"

"He just came to visit me."

"Was he asking a lot of questions?"

"Why should he, Raquel?" He fed her the opportunity to tell him the truth and waited.

She shrugged. "No special reason. He just seems like the sort of person who would ask a lot of questions." She changed the subject without subtlety.

"I have arranged something special for you today. About ten miles outside Gaza the Bedouins are giving a lunch for an Israeli officer who is leaving the district. I have arranged for you to be invited."

"You seem to have an entrée to a lot of things in Israel," Bartlett said. Again he waited; but she didn't elaborate.

The air was becoming hotter and he could smell the desert,

clean and dry, in his nostrils. Old excitements stirred. He wished they were going south to the burned and razored mountains veined with green wadis—to the wilderness in which Moses wandered—where he had worked a decade ago. But there wasn't time.

Raquel drove quickly and competently. Past the orange groves and refugee camps of Gaza; past its mud-hut poverty and its expensive taxis.

Bartlett said: "Why does a place like Gaza have such luxurious cabs?"

"It's where all the smuggling is done. And, of course, the United Nations were here."

"Meaning?"

"That they've got the money to support taxis."

"You don't think much of the United Nations?"

"Would you?" Raquel said. "If the United Nations hadn't withdrawn there wouldn't have been a Six Day War."

"But they're trying to do their best now, aren't they?"

"If they are," Raquel said, "I wouldn't like to be around when they weren't trying." She hooted a herd of goats off the road. "Did you see the observers up on the Golan Heights driving around in their cars? What good are they doing there?—there's hardly any shooting. Yet on the cease-fire line on the Jordanian border where there's shooting every day there's not an observer to be seen. Why? Because the Jordanians won't have them on their side, that's why. Not that it matters because they don't do any good when they are around. Look at the Suez Canal. Every day the shooting gets worse. And do you know how they have to negotiate a cease-fire?"

"Through some sort of telephone or radio link, I suppose," Bartlett said.

"Nothing as simple as that. The observers on the Egyptian side have to get in touch with Cairo and the observers on our side have to get in touch with Tel Aviv. Then Cairo and Tel Aviv get in touch with each other. I ask you—what is the point of them being there? And when they get wounded this side of the Canal Israeli troops have to rescue them while the Egyptians continue shooting."

Bartlett resolved to keep off the subject of the UN. The crops were becoming sparser now as they neared the end of the Gaza Strip and as they passed a refugee camp Raquel accelerated.

"What's the rush?" Bartlett said.

"It's a favourite spot for the schoolgirls."

"Do you mean they might shoot us?"

"Stone us," Raquel said. "Although one of them *was* arrested the other night for throwing percussion grenades near the police station. Her boyfriend persuaded her to do it."

Bartlett wondered how things were in the main street of Lewes, Sussex.

When they were outside the strip and the desert was permed with dunes Bartlett told her about the phone call from the President of the United States. She listened with quiet intensity.

Then she said: "How do you know it was him?"

"Because he was introduced as the President. Because the Ambassador called him the President and because I recognised his voice."

"It could have been a hoax."

"No. Why hoax me, for heaven's sake?"

She thought about that for a couple of minutes. They passed an Arab with two camels laden for market and turned right down a dirt road feeling its way through looming dunes. The breeze nosing among the dunes was hot and loaded with dust. Bartlett loved it all.

Raquel stopped to tie a scarf round her hair. Now, Bartlett thought, was the time for confessions. He glanced at her face, her eyes were screwed up against the sun. She looked worried. He imagined the conflicting loyalties with which she was contending—Israel and him.

Finally she said: "So you didn't understand what the call was all about?"

"Not at the time. I got the vague impression that they were

141

talking about the Ambassador in the third person at one stage. I was pretty confused and I was in a hurry and I was expecting to hear my wife's voice. Now of course I realise that they were talking about me."

"Why do you realise that?"

"I should have thought the answer was fairly obvious—ever since I overheard that conversation a lot of people have tried to kill, kidnap, or rob me."

"Perhaps they are trying to stop you repeating whatever you heard."

"Why should the Arabs and the Russians do that?"

"I don't know." Her face was tense. "I suppose you must have some knowledge that the Arabs and the Russians want to get hold of."

"And the Americans," he said. "Let's not forget Everett. And now Ralston, I suppose."

"You think he is a spy?"

"I think a lot of things these days that would never have occurred to me before."

"I suppose you are right." She restarted the engine and they bounced off towards the sea. "Thomas."

"Yes?"

"Do you love me?"

"I'm very fond of you," he said.

"But do you love me?"

He looked at her hands on the driving wheel. Very small, very hard. "Perhaps," he said.

"Why can't you answer me properly?"

Why can't you be honest with me? he thought. It was, after all, his life that was in danger. "Are you being perfectly honest with me?"

She didn't bother to look surprised. "I wish you had said you loved me." He began to speak but she stopped him. "We're there," she said. "Is it not beautiful?"

It was, he thought. The advance of the dunes was stopped by the wind from the sea and the last of them fell away steeply to the beach. To their left the beach swept away towards Suez, soft-sanded and laced with waves. On their right was a grove of bearded palm trees straying down to the waves. The sea was brochure blue.

The last of the Bedouins were arriving by camel. They sat cross-legged under a long, camel-hair awning supported by sticks. They smoked continuously and their teeth were as brown as their lined faces beneath their white headdresses.

Bartlett shook hands with one of the four sheikhs giving the lunch. He was a plump and happy man and over his robes he wore a double-breasted jacket as long as an overcoat bearing a label *Superfine quality worsted made in England.*

Raquel motioned to him to sit down beside a long carpet running the length of the improvised tent. She sat beside him. Beside them a Bedouin with an autumn-leaf face took sips of smoke from a cigarette held between three fingers.

Raquel said: "He is probably not as old as he looks. They all suffer from dehydration, you see. They should have ten litres of water a day but they only get about two. It's my job to try and make sure that they get more."

"Why are you so interested in the Bedouins?"

"Because they are our responsibility now."

"And you want their co-operation, I suppose."

Raquel said: "Already you look for other motives. Why cannot you accept that we do this for their good? We feed them too, you know."

"I believe you," Bartlett said. "But you get help, don't you?"

"Sure. CARE sends us food from the States."

Bartlett wondered if this was the opportunity to coax the truth from her—while their only companion was one Bedouin ancient absorbed with his cigarette. "Israel gets more aid from America than anywhere else, doesn't it?"

"Of course," Raquel said.

"Is there any aspect of your own work in which you don't co-operate with the Americans?"

She stared at the glittering sea; her features were strained.

143

After a few moments she said: "There are some aspects, I suppose."

He didn't know what she had been about to say. In any case it was too late. Other Bedouins sat around them and a bespectacled Israeli officer in a fawn shirt and a girl soldier sat opposite them. The girl had difficulty crossing her legs and revealed pink panties instead of the khaki issue that Bartlett had somehow expected. An Israeli major spoke to her angrily and she sat sideways with her legs tucked underneath her—her face blushing the colour of her pants.

Raquel said: "He was quite right—it upsets the Bedouins."

"Not only the Bedouins," Bartlett said.

They ate with their right hands from great trays of rice and mutton, and drank mineral waters. The sheikhs made speeches, thanking the departing Israeli officer for his help, asking if the Bedouins could work in Israel and seek more financial aid. The Israeli orators replied without commitment and warned the Bedouins about harbouring terrorists.

It was very hot under the camel-hair ceiling and the speeches in Hebrew and Arabic had a powerful soporific effect on Bartlett. Outside the Bedouin children were finishing off the remains of the food. He stared at the sea and found its gentle movement a powerful ally to the speeches. His head jerked forwards.

He was awoken by the puny shrilling of his wrist watch. The time for the confrontation had arrived. He wished that she had spoken first.

"Raquel," he said.

"Yes, Thomas?"

"I know all about you," he said.

As he spoke the Bedouins began to get to their feet and the children slid down the last sand dune on to the beach as if they wore skis.

"They are going to have camel racing on the beach for us," she said.

"Did you hear what I said?"

She nodded sadly.

"Come on then, we'll watch the camel racing together away from the rest of the crowd."

The camels didn't share their riders' enthusiasm for racing. A Bedouin fired a pistol and one camel moved lethargically forward; the other four watched it contemptuously.

"They are very lazy animals," Raquel said.

"I said I know all about you."

"I know. I heard you. But I do not think you know all about me. Perhaps not even I know that."

"I know you are an Israeli agent and that your assignment is to keep tabs on me. Was it so from the very beginning?" If only she would say no, he thought.

But she didn't. "From the very beginning," she said. "It was arranged that we should sit next to each other on the plane."

"And has it all been your job? Everything that has happened since?"

She shook her head and stared at the recalcitrant camels. A warm breath of air stirred her fringe. Behind them a helicopter hopped the dunes noisily.

"That's very difficult to believe."

"All right I don't ask you to believe it. But I tell you that it was not all my job. My God"—she turned to him angrily— "did I expect that I would fall in love with an English geologist of all people?"

The reference to love warmed his soul; he wished he could believe it; but even at the end she hadn't told him the truth. "You could have told me," he said.

"Told you? Do you think I am crazy already?" Her eyes were moist and the cobweb creases at their corners showed up beneath the dust. "How could I betray my country? My faith? Do you not think that I was tortured by it? But you must see that the future of my country comes before everything?"

"Perhaps if you had told me we could have worked something out."

"Perhaps you would have put your country first."

"I can hardly see that Britain comes into it."

"Britain is one of the four powers concerned . . . in any case this was information that Israel needed for herself. How was I to know whether or not you would pass the information on to the Americans?"

"But America is your ally. Your backer."

"That does not mean that our secret service works with theirs. Or anyone else's for that matter. We have the best intelligence system in the world—the Shin Beit. Why should we work with anyone else?"

"Because you haven't the largest," Bartlett said.

Down on the sandy straight beside the lace waves the camels were lining up again. This time a sheikh fired the pistol in the hope that the camels would be impressed by his person. They all moved off sideways in a crablike shambles. Faster this time but in different directions.

"We give information to no one," Raquel said. "We have learned our lessons." She paused. "What is going to happen now?"

"I don't know. It's very sad. But I don't see why we should let it ruin the day."

"You don't see why we shouldn't let it ruin the day? My God! Don't you see that I've got to get information from you? How can we go on as before?"

"You were going to try and get information from me anyway." He picked up a fragment of pottery lying on top of the dune. "In fact you haven't been making much of a job of it, have you?"

"No." She lit a cigarette. "I have not done well. I tried to ask you once or twice but you never answered me properly. And it always seemed so deceitful." She brightened a little. "Perhaps you can tell me what I want to know now? Then we can continue as before?" She looked at him uncertainly.

"The maps?"

"Yes," she said. "The maps. I suppose you've known for

146

some time that it was the maps. Have you known for some time that I was supposed to be spying on you?"

"I suppose so. It had to be you, didn't it?"

"I suppose so."

Down by the waves the camels were under starter's orders once more. The last sand dune had become a grandstand for the Bedouins and their Israeli guests. Along the brink of the dune stood a few Israeli soldiers armed with captured Kalatchinikov rifles. One of them wore a yarmulke.

Bartlett showed her the piece of pottery he had picked up. "You know what this is, I suppose."

"Roman?"

He nodded. "I think we're standing on the site of a Roman fort."

"Will you give me those maps, Thomas?"

"Do you know why everyone wants them?"

She turned away from him. "I only know that they are very important to Israel. Something to do with negotiations with the Arabs."

"And that's all you know?"

"Yes," she said. "That's all I know."

Bartlett thought sadly: You're lying, Raquel. A breeze from the sea tucked her denim skirt—longer than usual for the benefit of the Bedouins—in between her legs. He would have liked to put his arm around her waist.

"And you expect me to hand over my maps on a feeble pretext like that?"

"Feeble? You say it's feeble? The future of my country could depend on those maps. It might not matter to you whether this land is occupied by Israelis or Arabs. It might not matter to you if we are all driven into the sea. We have been betrayed enough times by the West . . ."

"Please," he said. "Don't get hysterical."

Below them the camels were loping along as if they were deliberately arranging a dead heat.

"All right," she said. "All right, I'm sorry. But please—where are those maps?"

"You know I hid them," he said.

"I know, I know. We've tried to think of everywhere but we failed."

"We?"

"My colleagues. Most of them thought that you would have hidden them in some quaint place with your British sense of humour. The Garden of Gethsemane or the Dome of the Chain."

"Or the Rockefeller Museum."

"Where did you hide them, Thomas?"

"It was quaint all right," he said. "Rather cunning, too."

"Where?" she said. "Just tell me. Where?"

"And what will you do if I tell you?"

She frowned. "I shall have to tell my people." She dropped her cigarette end in the sand. "You see—I cannot really be dishonest with you."

"You haven't done too badly over the past few days."

"Where did you hide the maps?"

"In Yosevitz's room," Bartlett said. "It seemed to be the least likely place in the whole of Jerusalem."

The metal on the jeep was too hot to touch. It smelled hot, too. Hot and oily and vapoured with gasoline. She took the road between the dunes fast bumping him against the door.

"What's the hurry?" he said.

She didn't answer. At first she had been astounded, then alarmed, then amused. Then all three together. It was the nearest, Bartlett decided, that she would ever get to hysterics.

They lurched round a bend scaring a couple of camels waiting haughtily for their owners.

Finally she said: "You must be crazy leaving it in the Russian's room."

"He's a Polish Jew, actually."

"Yosevitz is working for the Russians. This could be a tragedy for Israel. Why didn't you give me those maps, Thomas?"

"Because you didn't ask for them."

"But you knew I wanted them. You knew who I was." Bartlett detected a sob in her voice.

"Frankly I didn't know what the hell was going on to start with. You could have told me."

She drove into deep sand on the side of the road. The wheels spun, gripped—and they were off again.

She said: "Whereabouts in his room did you hide them? Under his pillow?"

"No, under his carpet."

She whimpered. "We must get back there."

"Get back? Why?"

"To get the maps of course."

Bartlett grinned. So far everyone else had made the play. Yosevitz, Ralston, the Arab, Raquel. Now it was his turn.

She said: "I ask you—what are you grinning at? Do you think it is funny that my country may be faced with disaster? That it is all my fault?"

He put his hand on her knee. "Don't fret yourself," he said.

"What do you mean—don't fret myself?"

"I didn't leave the maps in Jerusalem."

The jeep stopped abruptly near the crossroads at which they had turned earlier that day. "Where are they then?"

"In a satchel in the jeep," Bartlett said. "Under your seat as a matter of fact. You're sitting on them."

Chapter 20

The first thing Ralston did after Bartlett left Jerusalem was to check out his destination with a contact at the garage which had supplied the jeep to Raquel Rabinovitz.

The contact, who was an Arab mechanic, said: "Why do you want to know this information?"

Ralston handed him 150 Israeli lira: "That's the only reason you need to worry about." He paused. "In fact they're friends of mine—I want to surprise them."

"That will be difficult," said the mechanic. He had fawning manners and an oily voice.

"Why?"

"Because I saw the pass that the girl has got. They are going to Kantara."

"Are you sure?"

"I would not lie to you," said the Arab.

"I hope for your sake that you haven't."

As Ralston left the garage a cab pulled up and Yosevitz got out. Everything about him was shiny—his damp hair, his sunglasses made for the ski slopes, his non-porous nylon shirt, his glowing cheeks and forehead.

Poor bastard, Ralston thought. Sometimes you had to hand it to the British—they had ways of doing things. Nevertheless, beneath the Pierrot's disguise, Yosevitz was still a professional. Efficient and dedicated.

Or was he so dedicated? Ralston wondered why Yosevitz had failed to move up behind him at the Wailing Wall and attempt the execution that he had almost certainly planned? Had the faith which he had been born into suddenly asserted itself at its fount?

Ralston backed into a coffee shop as Yosevitz walked across the sidewalk into the garage. He was wearing his jacket despite the heat. Because, Ralston knew, he had an automatic underneath. They never went far without their guns.

Ralston climbed into his own cab and told the driver to take him to the Damascus Gate where he had another meet with Brandon from the American Embassy. Brandon wouldn't be enthusiastic about letting Bartlett motor into the Sinai Desert with an Israeli agent. Nor was he. But there was no alternative.

He looked out of the window and saw an Israeli policeman standing outside a curio shop listening to a group of Arabs and a European tourist, all talking at the same time. He guessed that the tourist's pocket had been picked. Or perhaps someone had cut the strap of his camera and run off with it.

The policeman looked very young. He was dark and thin, and yet tough in the Israeli way, a toughness bred by necessity whatever the physical limitations. His face was patient beneath his peaked cap; his uniform wasn't very smart.

Ralston remembered his days on the beat in Chicago. At night in particular. The drunks, the bums, the car thieves, the junkies. And the night people who were his friends, from clubs, newspaper offices, restaurants; sweepers, cleaners, milkmen, cab drivers. Good honest days.

Then promotion to the plain-clothes department. And his involvement—through what had appeared to be a routine murder—in the capture of a Russian who had shot an American diplomat in an apartment high above the city. The call to Washington, the praise for efficiency and discretion. It was the latter quality that particularly impressed them. Promotion to this, the highest echelon of plain-clothes work, and an

151

education in dishonesty that relegated the escapades of the crooks he had once arrested to the nursery. Berlin, Geneva, Paris, Vietnam.

But all the time it had seemed to Ralston that he had managed to retain honesty of purpose if not method. A small diamond set in the cotton-wool of deceit. The West versus Communism, them versus us; scuffles of cunning that you hoped were contributing to a pattern that benefited Mankind. The small diamond had always been bright with that honesty of purpose. But not on this assignment. Politics and prestige. A formidable partnership that had clouded the diamond's polish.

On the sidewalk the policeman was smiling. So were the Arabs and the tourist. One of the Arabs had probably decided that he had "found" the tourist's pocketbook in the gutter. Property returned, complainant satisfied, Arab not punished but possibly deterred. A good cop. Ralston envied him.

The cab rounded a corner and Ralston lost sight of them. They drove past the Notre Dame de France and stopped outside the Damascus Gate. The tall, balding figure of Brandon was standing at the entrance. Ralston's depression deepened.

Brandon said: "You must be crazy. Just like you were crazy to let that guy Yosevitz follow you with a gun when you were coming to meet me this morning."

"Maybe," Ralston said. "What do you figure I should have done?"

Brandon shrugged his meaty shoulders. "Held him, I guess. Persuaded him to tell you where these goddamn maps are."

"Great," Ralston said. "Just great. How would you have justified holding a British geologist prisoner in his hotel room?"

"Bartlett would have played ball with you eventually. He's not against us after all."

They walked on the outside of the wall towards Herod's Gate.

After a couple of minutes Brandon said: "I suppose we are sure that he's not against us. He's not a Red, is he?"

Ralston said: "He's about as Red as Queen Elizabeth."

"I still think you're screwing up this whole operation," Brandon said.

Ralston stopped and took a picture of an Israeli soldier with an Uzi on one arm and a soldier girl on the other. Perhaps he might even be able to sell some of his pictures to a magazine. He said: "I don't care what you think, Brandon. Do I need to remind you about the order of our seniorities?"

"Jesus," Brandon said. "So now he's trying to pull rank."

"Right," Ralston said. "Now get this—you're Embassy Security. Nothing more. And if you play your cards like this you never will be anything more."

Brandon held up his hands. "Okay," he said. "So I'm sorry."

Ralston looked at him speculatively. Slow but dependable. A good man on the beat. He smiled and the depression began its exit.

Brandon said: "So what are you grinning about?"

Ralston shook his head. "Bartlett's out in the Sinai with this girl. Right?"

"Right," Brandon said.

"So here's what we've got to do," Ralston said.

Ralston went back to his hotel room after he had primed Brandon and checked his .45 police-issue Colt. At least it was a good honest sort of gun, he thought.

Chapter 21

Raquel Rabinovitz knew what she had to do as the jeep bowled on towards El Arish, Kantara, and the Suez Canal. The knowledge made her intensely sad but there was no alternative. At least she did not have to do it immediately; the rest of the day was theirs. What happened after that depended on Bartlett's capacity for understanding.

She glanced at him sitting beside her. Face deeply tanned now with only a few peelings of skin on the bridge of his nose. Even the peeling skin was endearing. They passed a group of soldiers hitching lifts in the opposite direction. Muscled, brown, and arrogant with their guns on their shoulders and their peaked desert caps. Pride gleamed inside her; but her love was reserved for the Englishman with the sensitive features and greying hair sitting beside her.

Bartlett said: "How on earth did you manage to get passes to go as far as Kantara?"

"My work," she said. "I really am an expert on soil irrigation, you know. There is an irrigation project south of Kantara north of the Gidi Pass. I have work to do there."

"And they'll let both of us into Kantara?"

"You're lucky," she said. "They will today because the Red Cross has arranged a truce. Arabs who were stranded by the June war are being exchanged across the Canal. Some had crossed the Canal to visit relatives this side, others had gone across to Egypt. So today there will not be any shooting. Not until the exchange is over anyway."

"And then they'll start killing each other again?"

"I'm afraid so."

"Do you Israelis really want a peaceful settlement?"

"Of course," she said. "We have everything to lose because of the fighting." She took one hand off the steering wheel and touched his arm. "If the fighting stopped I could perhaps stop this other work and just help the desert to blossom." Her thoughts accelerated into a peaceful future. "Perhaps we could work together, you and I. Would you like that, Thomas?"

"Perhaps," he said.

"Are you still angry with me?"

"I'm not angry. I wish you could have trusted me."

"We could explore the Sinai together. You have told me how you love it to the south. Where Rhutm grows in the wadis, where leopards roam the mountains."

"It's very beautiful," he said.

She continued the seduction. "Drive up Wadi Feiran perhaps. You studying the formation of the mountains while I find sites for boring wells."

She imagined them sleeping together in one of the guest rooms of St Catherine's Monastery and wondering if it would constitute blasphemy.

They stopped at El Arish for refreshment. Most of the sand-coloured buildings were pitted with scars. The rest were truncated or devastated. In the centre of the town where they sat drinking beer and eating peta stuffed with humus and cold French fries there was a red-painted restaurant called the Cafe of Peace.

Their cafe was packed with troops. Jeeps and half-tracks stood outside. Men and machines exuded a triumphant virility. It was contagious. Despite her sadness Raquel revelled in the swagger around her. The soldiers smelled of sweat and oil and cordite. They wore sand goggles and their faces were powdered with dust. She studied them; bank clerks, surveyors, waiters, accountants, shopkeepers. And she thought of the man she had been going to marry. She was silent for a few minutes; then she touched Bartlett's hand. He smiled at her as he gulped at his glass of ice-cold Gold Star.

She said: "There was a big battle here." She pointed towards the sea. "The Egyptian officers were having beautiful houses built on the beach. Once upon a time it was a rest centre for the British."

"We rested everywhere," Bartlett said.

Across the table a huge soldier who looked like Fidel Castro winked at her. His interest only enhanced her tenderness for Bartlett who had none of the characteristics which she had imagined she admired in a man. Except bravery. But with Bartlett it seemed as if everything was shared. The desert, the hot sky, the rustle of the wind in the palms. She wished he could share the Israeli triumph with her.

He bought two more beers and gestured around the small, hot cafe. "I don't give much for the Arabs' chances."

"They have no chance," she said.

"I feel a little incongruous here. Only John Wayne's missing at the moment."

She wanted to kiss him. "You are not incongruous. I cannot imagine you being incongruous anywhere."

"Not even in the ladies' changing rooms?"

"You were not incongruous in the ladies' changing room at El Hamma."

She would ask him once more to let her have the maps, she thought. When they were on the road to Kantara. If he refused again she would have to act before they reached the Canal in case he had some crazy idea about handing the maps over to the United Nations. Which was as bad as handing them over to the Arabs or Russians.

Bartlett stood up and said: "Shouldn't we be on our way?"

"I suppose so."

But she didn't really want to go because the road might lead to the end of the sharing.

"Come on then."

He walked out of the cafe. Different in his slacks and bush shirt, but not incongruous. She followed him aware of the gaze of Fidel Castro and his colleagues.

Outside Bartlett bought her a necklace of tiny shells threaded on string from one of the Arab stalls.

"How much did that cost you?" she said. She was aware it was an Israeli question.

"You shouldn't ask."

"How much?"

"One Israeli pound."

"You were robbed." She put the necklace on. "But I shall always keep it."

They drove beside long deserted sands and telegraph-pole palms and long waves moving in slowly as if they were pulled on thread.

Bartlett said: "Back home ten thousand people crowd onto a stretch of sand half a mile long."

"I wouldn't advise it here," Raquel said.

"Why's that?"

"Because it's probably mined already."

Soon, she thought, she would have to ask him for the last time. When they reached the outskirts of Kantara.

They drove on through desert and scrub. Past skeletons of trucks and tanks. Past a rusting ammunition train perforated with holes like a colander when its fright had exploded. Past resting camels, leaning palms, and sleeping Arabs.

About fifteen miles before Kantara they were stopped at a roadblock beside a tented Army camp. Raquel showed her pass. The Israeli soldier, cigarette in mouth, looked curiously at Bartlett.

Raquel said in Hebrew: "He's going to help me find more water for all of you."

The soldier, who looked about eighteen, grinned and said: "Any cigarettes?"

She gave him a pack. He waved them on. Eight miles later she said: "Thomas, will you let me have those maps?"

157

"I was wondering when you were going to ask."

"Will you?"

"Perhaps. Not now."

"But you love me. Why cannot you give them to me now?"

"It's difficult to explain," Bartlett said. "It has nothing to do with my feeling for you. It has a lot to do with being made a fool of. Yosevitz, Ralston, that thieving Arab, and you. You've all tried to make a fool of me. I don't intend to part with the maps now. I've given my word."

"You've given your word? Who have you given your word to?"

"To Ralston I'm afraid."

The knowledge of what she now had to do settled heavily upon Raquel. Like fear, like sickness. "Why did you make such a promise to Ralston?"

"Why not? It's quite true that I don't intend to help the Arabs or the Russians."

"Or the Israelis?"

"I didn't say that."

"Give me the maps, then."

"Can you tell me why everyone wants them?"

"No," she said, "because I don't know." She looked away towards the serried skyline of broken buildings so that he could not see the lie on her face.

"I don't believe you."

"So be it," she said. With one hand she picked up his hand and kissed it. "So be it, my Thomas." She pushed her foot down on the accelerator and the jeep leaped forward towards the ruined city of Kantara.

From a distance of one mile Kantara appeared to have been devastated.

But as they got nearer they saw the occasional building still standing nursing its war wounds. Of humanity there was no sign.

They passed a dry, overgrown park with a dead fountain in the middle. Signs swinging in front of heaps of rubble that

158

had been cafes and shops; a scarred house of comparative dignity lonely behind a line of gum trees; empty streets with grass already invading through the cracks. A couple of dogs with herring-bone ribs barked at them feebly. There was a smell of putrefaction in the air.

Raquel looked anxiously around. She didn't want to get as far as the battered hotel where the United Nations were billeted. She stopped the car and pointed ahead at a shell-torn church. "That's the Coptic Church," she said. "We gave permission for it to be rebuilt after the June war. Then the Egyptians shelled it again."

"Where is everyone?" Bartlett said.

"We arranged for them all to be evacuated because of the shelling." She decided to emphasise the point. "Arabs shelling Arabs, you understand."

"I understand," he said. "Let's get on to the Canal."

Raquel considered the heavy pistol concealed beneath the oil rags beside her seat. Too big for a girl. But not for an Israeli girl. She drove slowly forwards.

They passed a terrace of ruined khaki-coloured houses to which a long verandah adhered. Perched on the verandah was an armchair, its upholstery ripped apart by a shell-splinter. A wall creaked in the imperceptible breeze.

"Why don't you get a move on?" Bartlett said.

She accelerated slightly.

They were just passing the Coptic Church when Raquel saw a jeep rattling towards them down a side street. She stopped their jeep.

"Why are you stopping?" he said.

She looked at him sadly.

The other jeep stopped at right angles to them. In it were a major and two soldiers in shirt sleeves. The major held a pistol in his hand and the two soldiers had Uzi submachine guns over their shoulders.

Raquel beckoned them over and spoke to the major in Hebrew.

Bartlett said: "What are you talking about?"

159

Raquel said: "I'm sorry, Thomas. We have to have those maps. I have told these men about the situation. In fact they knew we were coming here. You must have realised that I had to warn the Army about our approach."

Bartlett shrugged. "It hadn't occurred to me."

"Thomas," she said, "please forgive me."

"Get on with it," he said. "What are you going to do now?"

"We will go with them in their jeep to an Army post where there is an officer of Israeli intelligence. There we will hand over the maps to him. You see, I have no alternative, Thomas."

The major gestured with his pistol. He was very dark with a small moustache and taut features. "Please hurry up," he said.

Raquel nodded. "The maps," she said. "Please get them, Thomas."

Bartlett said: "Do you really think they are worth all this?"

"They are worth it to us," she said.

"Very well." He put his hand under Raquel's empty seat and brought out the satchel containing the maps. He handed it to Raquel.

The major waved his pistol again and said: "You'd better come with us."

"We'll follow you," Raquel said.

"No, please, you come with us. There are many mines about. If you even stray away from our tyre tracks you might blow yourselves up."

Bartlett said: "You'd better go with him whether there are any mines or not."

"Why?" Raquel said.

"Because if I'm not much mistaken that gentleman you've just handed the maps to is an Egyptian."

Raquel stood still, muscles tensed.

The two soldiers looked questioningly at the major.

Then Raquel leaped for the gun beside the driving seat. She knew it was hopeless but it was preferable to whatever the Arabs had in store for her. It was also preferable to failure.

She felt the butt of the gun beneath the rags. She was aware that Bartlett and the major were fighting behind her.

She felt a blow on the head and the hot blue sky darkened to dusk to night.

Chapter 22

Bartlett was lying on a beach and waves were falling across his face, drowning him. He tried to move his head to one side but pain illuminated by red light exploded inside him. When he finally opened his eyes the Egyptian was throwing water in his face. He stopped drowning, but the pain remained. He wanted to massage it away with his hands; but his hands were tied behind his back. He stopped struggling and lay on his back looking at the Egyptian.

The Egyptian said: "I'm sorry I had to hit you so hard but you were putting up a very good fight." His English was elaborate, his tone sarcastic. He pointed at his own puffed eye. "You did not look as if you had it in you."

Bartlett tried to speak but the pain gagged him.

The Egyptian said: "I wish I could give you something to ease the pain but we brought nothing like that with us." He looked beyond Bartlett. "Your girl friend is in better shape than you."

Bartlett managed to turn his head. Raquel lay beside him, hands and feet bound. Her face was pale but she was conscious. She said: "Hallo, Thomas."

Bartlett tried to speak. The words felt very thick. "Where are we?"

The Egyptian said: "In the ruins of a small hotel on the outskirts of Kantara where no one can find us."

Bartlett looked at the wall. There was a shellhole the size

of a coffee table in it. It was burned black at the edges and the haphazard brickwork was exposed.

The Egyptian saw where he was looking. "Those bricks —bad workmanship, I'm afraid. But, bad though it is, it belongs to us. As does the Sinai." He glanced at Raquel. "As does the whole of Palestine."

"Israel," she said.

The Egyptian smiled. "She has courage that one. But so do most Israelis. I should know—I was brought up there."

Bartlett said nothing.

The Egyptian said: "We have a little time. I will answer any obvious questions to save you the effort of speaking." He lit a cigarette. "I was ten when Palestine was handed over to the Jews. My father had to stay behind because he was sick— he had been a strong and proud man. I inherited his pride. I decided I would never be a second-class citizen and I would never give up the fight. When I was fifteen I managed to cross the border. I went to Cairo because I believed that was the true centre of the Arab world."

Bartlett spoke very slowly. "You speak very good English," he said. The pulses of pain were coming a little slower.

"The Egyptians realized my worth. A dedicated Arab Nationalist. Hebrew-speaking with a good knowledge of Palestine. They must also have thought I was intelligent because they gave me the best education possible. That is how I come to speak English. Yamani is my name, by the way."

Bartlett realised that he was in the presence of a man very much in love with himself. As he was entitled to be. Handsome, strong, intelligent. The Arabs could do with a few more like him.

Raquel said to him: "If you are caught you will be shot as a spy."

Yamani laughed. "Very true. But then you are a spy as well. You have been spying on this man Bartlett for a long time."

"He knows about it," she said.

"Very touching," Yamani said. He knelt and allowed them

163

each a smoke of his cigarette. "You are probably wondering how we got here?"

Bartlett shrugged because he didn't want to fuel the Arab's ego. But it didn't need fuel.

Yamani said: "Cairo was informed from Tel Aviv that you were probably heading in this direction. During the night while an artillery duel was in progress we crossed the Canal. That is not an uncommon practice. But this time we came wearing Israeli combat dress."

Raquel said: "You will be caught."

"I think not," he said. "This morning on the radio we received confirmation that you were on your way. It was very simple to hide in the ruins of Kantara and await your arrival. Especially with the Israeli Army and the United Nations concentrating on the exchange of refugees. It will be even easier for us to get back across the Canal. The Israelis will not be looking for Arabs crossing in that direction."

Raquel said: "But the Egyptians will. Perhaps *they* will shoot you."

He shook his head. "They will be warned that we are coming." He turned his attention to Bartlett again. "Are you impressed with our efficiency on this occasion?"

"I'm impressed with your self-satisfaction."

"You think I am a conceited man?"

"You are not bashful," Bartlett said.

The smile faded a little. "It is time more of my people found their pride. We have wallowed in our inferiority complex for too long."

Raquel said: "That is only natural because you are inferior."

He pretended to ignore her. "But the spirit is changing. All along the borders with Israel you will see it. From the oldest Fedayeen down to the youngest Ashbal. Soon no force on earth will be able to stop us. This is not just a struggle for land, Mr Bartlett, this is Jihad—a Holy War."

Bartlett said: "You have already been beaten by the Jews three times."

"We will not be beaten the fourth time." His composure was

164

feeling the strain. "Next time we will drive the Jews into the sea."

"I don't think they will go," Bartlett said.

"Why not?"

Bartlett glanced at Raquel and managed to smile.

Yamani said again: "Why not?"

"Because, as I understand it, they're not very fond of swimming."

The Arab stubbed out his cigarette viciously. "Make the most of your famous British sense of humour. You have not much longer in which to enjoy it."

Raquel said: "What are you going to do with us?"

"We have the maps," he said. "In particular one map. Unfortunately for Mr Bartlett he knows its content. Therefore he will have to be killed. And I'm afraid you will have to join him. You are, after all, an officer in Israeli Intelligence." He paused. "And now I'm afraid I must leave you."

He called out in Arabic and one of the other two commandos came in, Uzi at the ready. Bartlett and Raquel were left looking up the barrel of a squat, efficient Israeli-made submachine gun.

Through the jagged hole in the wall Bartlett watched the dark blue of the sky begin to fade. Soon the outlines of the dunes in the desert would be softened by dusk, their hollows filled with mauve shadows.

He looked around their quarters. A small reception desk covered with dust and plaster; a punctured armchair which looked as if it had once been British Army married quarters issue; a photograph of Nasser perforated by a bullet hole on the wall; a greasy sofa under the shellhole. Through an arch he could see a few chairs and broken tables.

A sour dirty smell pervaded the place. The smell of death.

The Arab guard sat behind the desk, a bizarre and burly receptionist in a dead hotel. He put his submachine gun on the desk and stared at them without expression. A big brown man with a wrestler's physique, jagged teeth, and a freshly healed wound down his cheek. The scar pulled slightly at one eye adding menace to his gaze.

Raquel said: "I'm sorry, Thomas."

"I should bloody well think you are," Bartlett said.

"Do you hate me?"

Bartlett said: "I hardly think this is the time or the place to discuss our future relationship. As far as I can see we haven't got a future let alone a relationship." The pain came at much longer intervals now.

"We must escape," Raquel said.

"An excellent suggestion," Bartlett said. "How?"

"First," she said, "we must discover if this man speaks English."

"Insult him in English then."

Raquel insulted him with fluency and feeling.

Bartlett said: "I didn't know you knew words like that." He felt shocked; his shock amused him.

"I'm sorry about the language. A few phrases I picked up in New York. But you see he doesn't understand them. So we can talk freely."

"What do you want to talk about? How is your head by the way?"

"My head's all right," she said. "They didn't hit it very hard. The trouble is we can't do much until it's dark. Not in front of this fat pig."

The Arab traced a picture in the dust with one finger.

"I should imagine he's drawing a gallows," Bartlett said.

"Always you joke," she said. "I think that you are now entitled to an explanation. The reason why everyone wants those maps? Or that one map, rather."

Bartlett savoured the moment. He was deeply fond of her; nevertheless he had been looking forward to this. "I know why everyone wants it," he said. He watched her face in the mellowing light; it was rewarding.

"You know?"

"I told you once that I thought I had an idea."

166

"But I didn't believe you. In fact I don't know that I believe you now. What is the reason?"

"Oil," he said.

"Ah." She thought about it, a little puzzled, a little awed. "How long have you known that?"

"Not all that long. In fact I've been pretty slow. But you see there was no reason in the first place why it should occur to me. People trying to kill me, people trying to steal my briefcase. I suppose you think the answer should have been obvious then. But there was a lot more in that briefcase than just maps. They could have been after anything."

"But you don't know the whole story."

"I'm sure I don't," he said.

"You just know it's oil?"

"That's all I know. I don't understand the in-fighting." He had a pretty good idea but he wanted the full explanation from her.

"Those maps," she said. "When were they made?"

"Some go back to 1869. There was an Ordnance Survey of part of the Sinai then."

"And the others?"

"All different times. But I suppose the map you're interested in is the one drawn up in the surveys immediately after the First World War."

She moved her head in the dust in confirmation. "I believe a German was put in charge of a team whose sole task was to find likely sites for oil in the Sinai."

"You're absolutely right," Bartlett said. The pain was coming much less frequently now. He wished they were sitting up because talking on the floor made the words sound incongruous. "The whole team perished when their truck broke down near Bir Hasane." He tried to move his hands behind his back but they were bound very tightly. "Is this the time for this discussion? I rather feel that we should be working out methods of escaping."

"We can't do anything until dark," she said.

167

"And then what can we do?"

"I don't know."

"That's great," he said. "Absolutely marvellous."

"We might as well talk," she said. "It keeps our minds occupied. There is nothing else we can do except hope that an Israeli patrol finds us."

"And there's not much chance of that," he said.

The "receptionist" picked up the Uzi and examined it with interest as if he hadn't used one before.

Raquel said: "I know about the German and his men. They had two trucks. One broke down and the Arabs drove away in the other."

"Correct." Bartlett tasted plaster and smelled the sour odour of death. There was probably a body in a cellar. He said: "I found the bones of the German and the others when I came to the Sinai years later. Although I suppose you know that."

"I know," she said. "I suppose you know how I found out."

He said with a weariness that had nothing to do with their plight: "Through my wife, I suppose. Although there was no secret about it."

"You also told her about the map. The sketch map that the German made while he was dying. It was the only map in existence that gave the sites where there might be oil inland from the Gulf of Suez. Why, Thomas, did you have to tell your wife about the existence of such a map just before you were coming to Israel?"

"Quite frankly it didn't seem to matter. The Egyptians have never bothered very much about the oil potential of the Sinai in the past."

"They have on the Gulf," she said. "Ras Abu Rudeis, for instance, south of the manganese mines. But they haven't done much about it farther inland." She paused. "Do you love me, Thomas?"

He wanted to kiss her dry cracked lips. He nodded.

"Say it then."

"I love you."

She smiled and the smile reached him and warmed him.

She said: "They didn't do anything more about the oil potential because they are, after all, Arabs. What have they ever done with the desert? It is we Israelis who make it bloom."

"All right," Bartlett said. "Forget the propaganda for a bit."

"We need to know where that oil is," Raquel said. "Who wants to give oil to Jews these days? We have enough trouble getting arms from you let alone oil. If we had enough in the Sinai it wouldn't matter to us if no one wanted to give us any."

"And you reckon one of those maps of mine can do the job for you?"

"So do the Arabs and Russians. And the Americans—but their reasons are a little more complicated than ours."

"Impossible," Bartlett said.

"They are much more complicated," she said. "That's why the President of the United States was on the phone. Unfortunately you weren't the only one to overhear the call."

"I don't understand," Bartlett said.

"It's very simple. The United States wants peace in the Middle East. Make no mistake about that. They also want to be the boss—just as the Russians do. So they want all the cards. And they want the prestige of being the country than puts forward the formula for peace at the four-power talks. You can't blame them."

"I see," Bartlett said. And he almost did. "You mean a settlement based on a withdrawal by the Israelis."

Raquel said quickly: "A limited withdrawal from the Sinai only. But to agree to that we've got to know where the oil is. We don't want to pull out from territory oozing with oil which the Arabs can exploit. Whoever produces the formula for peace has *got* to know where those sites are."

Bartlett said: "What have your own geologists and petrologists been doing since the June war?"

He thought wistfully of what they should have been doing. The search for outcroppings indicating alternating layers

169

of porous and impermeable sedimentary rock, particularly when it was uplifted into domes or anticlines. And the latest geophysical techniques employing magnetic, seismic, and gravitational theories.

Raquel said: "Are you listening to me, Thomas?"

He returned to the hotel. "Yes," he said.

"I don't think you were. I was pointing out that the June war never really finished for us. We have been fighting ever since. We've done some prospecting for oil but it's very difficult under such circumstances."

Through the shellhole Bartlett watched the first star materialise. Their guard stood up and spoke in Arabic.

"What's he saying?" Bartlett said.

"I think he's worried that he can't see us properly."

The Arab picked her up and sat her on the sofa in front of the shellhole. Then he put Bartlett next to her so that he could see both their silhouettes. He returned to his desk and lit a cigarette. In the light of the match Bartlett saw one drooping eye staring at him.

The Arab put out the match and Bartlett felt behind him for the satchel left there after the maps had been removed. It was open. His hands had been tied so that the palms and fingers faced outwards. He touched trowel, hammer, knife. He felt the knife's blade with his thumb. Somehow he had to wedge it so that he could rub the rope binding his wrists against it.

He manipulated the knife for a couple of minutes until the handle was stuck through the buckle of the satchel. Then he began to work the rope against the cutting edge. Sweat gathered on his forehead and trickled into his eyes. His breathing gathered speed.

"What are you doing?" Raquel said.

"Shut up," he said in a quiet, casual voice. "The receptionist may know a few words of English." Then he whispered, "I'm trying to cut the rope."

He rubbed away, waiting to feel the first fibres breaking. But nothing happened.

170

The guard spoke again in Arabic.

Bartlett said: "What's he on about now?"

"He's asking why your breathing is so quick."

"Tell him I've got a fever. Tell him I caught malaria in the Congo. Tell him anything."

Raquel managed a few phrases of Arabic. The guard grunted as if he were satisfied.

The light through the shellhole was silver from the moon and the stars. He thought of the wild red desert frozen now on its chill glow. His wrists began to ache, then to burn. He had intended to have the knife sharpened for a long time.

As he sawed and suffered he contemplated the last decade of his life. Helen and her men. The first one and the sickness of discovery. His efforts at reconciliation interpreted as weakness and acquiescence.

Ever since his arrival in Israel they had diagnosed weakness. Yosevitz the Polish Jew, Everett the dead American, the thieving Arab in Jerusalem, Ralston with his detective ways. And probably Raquel.

They had all presumed too much. Bartlett smiled in the glacial darkness despite the pain burning his wrists as if someone were holding a candle flame to them. He would escape: if he didn't then he deserved to die because they were right— he was weak.

Still he couldn't detect any give in the thin, nylon rope. Or could he?

The first strand seemed to break as the first shell exploded in Israeli-held Kantara. The foyer of the hotel was lit briefly with orange and white light. The crack of the explosion followed almost immediately and the brickwork in the shellhole grated uneasily.

Raquel said: "You see who starts it?"

Bartlett stopped sawing for a moment. "You never give up, do you?" he said.

"Why do you say that? It is quite plain—they have started the shooting." Bartlett imagined her shrugging with contemptuous eloquence.

171

The guard paced the foyer restlessly.

Raquel said: "He is very upset. I do not think the Egyptians were supposed to start shooting just yet. But they get everything wrong."

Bartlett began to work again. He looked at Raquel's luminous watch. It was 8 P.M. He guessed that Yamani would be back soon.

The ground shook with the detonations of heavy artillery. Shells ruining ruins. Explosions of raucous, monotonous futility. And still he could not sever the thin nylon rope with the blunt knife. The pain in his wrists told him he couldn't continue much longer.

Shells, mortars, rockets. Through the shellhole in the wall he saw tracers crayoning the sky. The walls moved, the ruptured earth protested. Then the sharper bark of the Israeli artillery mounted on Sherman tanks answering the Egyptian guns.

Raquel said: "The shooting by the Egyptians was bound to happen, I promise you."

"Why? Because it happens every night?"

"Not just that. Because of the refugees as well. As soon as refugees have been exchanged the Egyptian guns always start up."

He rested because he had no alternative. The sweat was icy beneath his bush shirt. "Don't the Israelis ever start it?"

"Ask the United Nations."

A shell exploded so close that rubble and slivers of shell-casing peppered the walls and roof of the hotel.

The guard picked up his Uzi and went to the door. He swore succinctly in Arabic and returned to the desk.

"What do they propose to do with us?" Bartlett said. He had started sawing again.

"Kill us, I suppose. Just like Yamani said. Do you feel frightened, Thomas?"

"Scared stiff," he said. He was pleased with his voice because it belied the fear he felt.

"I wish I could kiss you."

"I wish so, too."

"I think that he will probably leave an explosive charge here because he will not want Israeli soldiers to find us here with bullet holes in us."

"That's very reassuring," Bartlett said.

As he spoke a shell exploded outside the gap in the wall. The detonation fired arrows of pain into the eardrums. It was louder than Bartlett had imagined anything could be. Part of the wall collapsed and he heard metal flying around him.

He also heard metal strike flesh and bone. The guard cried out once. A thin high-pitched scream that sounded alien to his physique.

The sounds and sensations faded.

"Raquel," he said.

"Yes?"

"Are you all right?"

"I'm all right. Are you, Thomas?"

"Yes, I'm all right."

But he knew that Raquel and he were the only people alive in the ruins of the hotel on the devastated outskirts of the old Arab town of Kantara.

Bartlett said: "You can move closer to me now and have a go with this knife." Her wrists were still bound but if they sat back-to-back, she would be able to saw against the rope.

The big guns were still firing. Occasionally he heard a stuttering bark which Raquel identified as a Gruyanov wheel-mounted machine gun firing from the Egyptian side.

She edged along the sofa. Halfway across she stopped.

"What is it?" he said.

"A shell splinter," she said. "It's hot." He heard her gasp. Then she was beside him cutting at the rope around his wrists with the jagged sliver of shell-casing.

"Is it very hot?"

"Yes," she said, and he heard the wince in her voice. One strand of the rope parted, then another. A Katyusha

173

rocket exploded nearby and he heard the crash of falling masonry.

"The other two Arabs will be back soon," he said.

"I'm doing my best," she said.

The shell splinter was sawing into his flesh but he said nothing. Her breath was rapid. He saw her face, marble-white in the exploding light, and kissed her. He felt the blood from his wrists flowing down his fingers. He hoped she was nowhere near the artery.

He said: "When you've freed my hands I'll get the guard's gun from the desk."

"No," she said, "I know how to use it."

"No," he said. "I'll get it."

"Why?"

"I can't explain. But it has to be me." He didn't know if he could stand the pain in his wrist much longer without crying out.

A ruined house across the road was burning and the hotel foyer was lit by its flames.

Raquel said: "You're bleeding. I didn't know . . ."

"Just don't stop," he said.

Over his shoulder he could see the shell splinter she was wielding catching the light from the flames. Smoke hung in one heavy layer. The artillery duel continued. Bartlett remembered how he had anticipated witnessing the newspaper headlines jerking into life like marionettes . . .

Another strand broke and he forced his wrists apart. The blood was flowing freely from the wounds. He continued the outward pressure with his hands. A snap and they were free.

At the same moment the door swung open and the other Arab under Yamani's command stood there, Uzi at the ready. He spoke rapidly in Arabic.

"What's he saying?" Bartlett said.

"I don't know. Something about Yamani coming back."

Then the Arab saw the body of his colleague slumped over the reception desk. The shell splinter had opened up the back of his skull and the impact had split the tender scar on his face. His gun lay on the desk beside him.

The Arab cried out and ran to the body. As he turned it over Bartlett threw the hammer from the satchel. It hit the Arab on the side of the face with a crunch. His right hand reached for the butt of the Uzi; then he collapsed on the floor.

Bartlett ran across the foyer and knelt beside him. He was still breathing but very slowly. There was a dent at his temple where the hammer had struck him. Bartlett picked up the Uzi.

Raquel said: "Please, Thomas, give it to me. I know how to use it."

He shook his head. "I know how to press a trigger."

The flames across the road were reaching high into the shell-scarred night. Their light was incongruously mellow in the foyer and shadows pranced on the walls.

Raquel took his hands and looked at the wounds. "I'm sorry," she said.

Bartlett said: "So you should be." He picked up the gun again. "Yamani will be back any minute. We'll have to surprise him. I'll get behind the door. You stay over on the sofa."

"We must get the map," she said.

"To hell with the bloody map."

"No," she said. "Not to hell with the bloody map. I must have it. Israel must have it."

"I said to hell with the bloody map. Now you get over there while I wait behind the door."

"All right, Thomas."

Through the shellhole he saw tracer shells darning the sky. Then there was a pause in the shooting and all he could hear was the crackle of the flames across the road. After a few seconds the Gruyanov cleared its throat and barked again. And the big guns followed its lead.

Raquel sat quite still in the firelight. She said: "Thomas."

"Yes?"

"Will you ever forgive me?"

"I don't know."

"I had to do it."

"I know."

A Katyusha exploded nearby and the shellhole ground its bricks.

She said: "Thomas."

"Yes?"

"You have been very wonderful. I didn't believe you could be like this."

"Neither did I."

"You are as brave as any Israeli soldier."

He grinned in the shifting light. "That's praise indeed."

"I love you," she said.

"Good," he said. "Now just tell me how to fire this damn thing."

"Let me," she said.

"No. Just tell me."

But she didn't because at that moment they heard a jeep draw up. Bartlett tightened his grip on the gun. The engine stopped and they heard footsteps crunching on the rubble.

Chapter 23

The hotel manager said: "All we know, ma'am, is that he went out into the Sinai. We had expected to hear from him now."

Helen Bartlett who had called the manager directly put the receiver down. She knew now that her husband was in trouble. And she knew with a sickening certainty that it was her fault.

She went into the lounge and poured herself a gin-and-tonic. Then she put on her new summer coat and got the Singer Gazelle out of the garage.

She drove fast through the gathering darkness along roads still wet from the day's showers. Within two hours she was in the outskirts of London. She drove first to the American Embassy.

The duty officer said: "Hi there, Mrs Bartlett."

"Do you know where the Ambassador is tonight?" Helen Bartlett said.

"I guess he's at some cocktail party or other. I can't remember which one offhand."

"Can you find out for me, Joe? I'm supposed to be at a cocktail party tonight. The only thing I can remember about it is that the Ambassador was going there as well."

"I sure can, Mrs Bartlett. But you'll be kind of late, won't you?"

"Better late than never," Helen Bartlett said.

177

The duty officer checked on a diary. "He's at the West German Ambassador's home," he said.

"Thank you," Helen Bartlett said. "Thank you very much."

When she reached the German Ambassador's home the last guests were already leaving. She walked straight in and waited beside her husband's namesake who was talking to the French Ambassador.

The French Ambassador moved away. Ambassador Bartlett turned and noticed Helen Bartlett for the first time. Surprise hardened into suspicion on his tough, pouchy face.

"Good evening," he said. "Mrs Bartlett, isn't it? Is there anything I can do for you? If it's anything connected with your past employment perhaps you would be good enough to call at the embassy in the morning."

"It's got nothing to do with the fact that you had me fired," she said.

He fingered his pouches and sipped his Scotch. "What has it got to do with, Mrs Bartlett?"

In the elegant background a French security officer hovered uneasily.

"It's got to do with my husband. I think he's in trouble in Israel."

"But he's a British subject, Mrs Bartlett. Surely the British Foreign Office are the people to consult."

"No," she said. "Because you know what it's all about."

"I know nothing about geology."

"Have you got a drink?"

"I'm not the host but there still seems to be a hell of a lot of it around."

"A gin-and-tonic, please."

He beckoned a waiter and said: "Now please explain yourself, Mrs Bartlett."

She said: "I know why I was fired now. It was because of my association with a diplomat at the Jordanian Embassy, wasn't it?"

"Go on, Mrs Bartlett." His wife hovered at the door of

178

the room but he signalled to her to go away. There were now only about half a dozen guests left.

"You decided I was a bad security risk so you got rid of me. I don't blame you one little bit. But now I've put two and two together, Mr Ambassador. The diplomat from the Jordanian Embassy was interested in what I said about Tom's maps. I also talked about them at another of these damned parties. I guess your people must have been just as interested. Now Tom's in Israel and he's disappeared."

"Disappeared? Are you sure, Mrs Bartlett?"

"I couldn't get him on the phone just now. His hotel at Jerusalem said they had expected him to call. They said he was out in the Sinai Desert somewhere. And he's due to address the conference tomorrow."

"I shouldn't worry too much. There aren't too many telephones in the Sinai, you know. I reckon he'll ring his hotel when he finds one."

She drained her gin-and-tonic. "Be honest with me, Mr Ambassador, is Tom in some sort of danger because of me?"

"I think you're jumping to conclusions, Mrs Bartlett. I don't know what these maps are that you're talking about."

"You're lying," she said.

The Ambassador nodded at the French security officer. "I think it's about time you left," he said. "If you're really worried I recommend you to try your own Foreign Office." He finished his whisky. "It's a pity you didn't get around to worrying when you were consorting with your friend from the Jordanian Embassy. Or before that even."

"You've got to help me," she said.

"You look like a woman eminently capable of helping herself," he said. He put down his glass. "Good night, Mrs Bartlett." He walked out of the room.

Helen Bartlett started to follow him but the doorway was occupied by the security officer. "I think you'd better leave, ma'am," he said.

She nodded and felt the tears assembling in her eyes. "I'm going," she said.

In the car chagrin joined her fears for her husband. She thought: The bastards can't push me around like that. She drove towards Chelsea.

By the time she reached Sloane Square she had decided that perhaps the Ambassador was right—Tom would phone his hotel when it was possible.

She parked the car and had a drink at the Antelope. She noted a few glances of admiration from various men at the bar and wondered if any of them would try to pick her up.

She ordered one more gin to go with the remains of the tonic. Who the hell was Miss Rabinovitz? Perhaps she was in the desert with her husband. She knew what these Israeli girls were like.

She finished her drink and lingered a moment. But none of the men offered to buy her another.

She then drove to the mews near Kings Road where Ahmed lived.

He was just leaving with a girl with long fair hair and a silly haughty face.

Helen Bartlett called out to him. He opened the door of his red sports car and popped the girl inside. He smiled and said: "Why, good evening, Mrs Bartlett."

"Ahmed," she said, "I must talk to you."

"Sorry," he said. "Not now."

It had begun to rain and a few drops sparkled on his furry hair. He carried an umbrella and wore a white roll-collar shirt under a blue blazer.

"I've *got* to speak to you, Ahmed."

He smiled again and walked round the car. "Sorry, Mrs Bartlett, can't stop."

"But it's very important. That . . . that little tart can wait, can't she?"

He stopped smiling. "Go back to your husband, Mrs Bartlett. Although I don't know what he did to deserve you."

He slammed the door and the car moved off, sleek and aggressive in the thickening rain.

180

Helen Bartlett cried a little; then returned to the Antelope where one of the men at the bar offered to buy her a gin-and-tonic. Later they went back to the apartment in Marylebone High Street.

Chapter 24

Yamani kicked the door open and came in with a pistol in his hand. He looked at Raquel and the dead and the unconscious Arabs. Then Bartlett brought the butt of the Uzi down.

But Yamani's reflexes were jungle-quick. As the butt came down he swung up his arm defensively. His arm took most of the force of the blow and the pistol spun on to the floor.

Then Yamani was out of the door again. Through the shellhole they saw him running across the road towards the blazing building. Bartlett thrust the barrel of the Uzi through the shellhole and pulled the trigger. The bullets kicked up a hedge of dust behind him.

Then he was gone. Somewhere behind the flames. Bartlett sent another clutch of bullets into the flames, feeling the ugly power of the gun and smelling its smoke.

He said: "I'm sorry."

She said: "It couldn't be helped."

"He was very quick."

"You should have let me have the gun."

"I said I was sorry."

She smiled at him in the grotesque firelight. "I did not mean to criticise. It's just that I learned how to fire one of those guns."

"I thought you were a policewoman."

She ignored him. "Yamani won't go far," she said. "He

182

knows he's got to kill you because you know the contents of the map."

Bartlett laughed. "That damned map," he said.

"What are you laughing about?"

"I'll tell you later. Right now I have no intention of letting Yamani kill me."

"We've got to get the map," she said.

"Ah yes," he said. "The map. My map, in fact."

"You won't let me have it?"

"We'll see," he said. "After all I've got the gun."

She stood up suddenly keeping away from the shellhole. "Did Yamani have any grenades?"

"I don't remember," he said.

"Come on," she said. "We've got to get out of here."

She ran down a corridor, pulling his arm, and dragged him into one of the bedrooms facing away from the burning building. They fell across a bed which collapsed.

The explosion from the foyer was as loud as a shell-burst. The blast charged down the corridor kicking open the doors. The bedroom was lit with orange light.

Bartlett and Raquel allowed it all to subside, holding each other as tightly as the Uzi would permit.

Raquel said: "Good."

"Is it?"

"Yes, because he may think we're dead and come out of hiding. Although I think he is a very clever man. Anyway we must go back to the foyer."

"Supposing he lobs another grenade in?"

"He won't. That one would have killed us if we'd been in there."

They went stealthily back to the foyer. The reception desk had disappeared and small flames were investigating the sofa. The wall that had been holed by a shell was bulging outwards and swaying. The bodies of the two Arabs had been torn apart by the blast. Bartlett looked at them and felt a surge of vomit in his stomach.

He said: "You get back in the corridor."

"Why?"

"Just do as I tell you."

"I've seen bodies before."

"I don't give a damn about tough Israeli womanhood at the moment. You just get back in that corridor. It's no sight for a girl." He waved the Uzi at her.

"All right, Thomas. But you must get to the shellhole and watch for Yamani crossing the road."

"All right," he said. He stepped over the remains of the bodies trying to control the nausea.

The fire in the house was beginning to die. But the artillery duel wasn't. The big guns pumped away at each other and earth and sky leaped with their thunder and lightning. The devastation of devastation, the acme of human folly.

Bartlett crouched beside the shellhole, waiting. Above him the bulge in the wall grated and murmured.

The nausea subsided and he thought irrationally of Helen. If it hadn't been for her he wouldn't have been in Kantara because the trip to Israel had only been an escape. He decided, as he nursed a submachine gun waiting to kill a man, that he would never live with her again. The old Bartlett would have done: not the new.

He thought he noticed a movement to one side of the subsiding flames and gripped his gun tighter. A rocket exploded nearby; the wall protested more loudly.

This time there was a movement. Bartlett's finger caressed the trigger.

He saw Yamani as the wall collapsed. Raquel shouted from the corridor. He fired wildly and leaped backwards. The wall swung outwards and stood poised for a moment. Then crashed into the roadway.

Raquel shouted again. "Run, Thomas. Run."

He stumbled back towards her. Together they ran along the corridor through a door at the end. Outside they crouched at the base of a ravaged palm tree.

Raquel says: "He knows we're alive now. He'll be after us."

"Or we'll be after him," Bartlett said.

184

She looked at him in the radiance that was a fusion of moonlight, firelight, and shellfire. "Aren't you scared?"

"Yes," he said. "Just don't mention that damned map, that's all."

Bullets thudded into the palm tree two feet above their heads.

They lay still. Raquel said: "We must get behind some cover. I think he's only got a pistol."

"And some grenades."

"Come on," she said. "Keep low. Be quiet. When we get behind that wall over there we must work out a plan."

"Good," Bartlett said. "As long as Yamani hasn't got a better one."

On the other side of the Canal the Gruyanov barked erratically. Behind the machine guns the heavy Russian artillery kept up the barrage.

As he dodged through the ruins on his way back to the jeep Bartlett wondered what stage the United Nations ceasefire negotiations had reached. Calls to Tel Aviv and Cairo, calls between Tel Aviv and Cairo, then perhaps a break for rearmament.

He found the jeep where the Arabs had left it. The heavy pistol and ammunition were beside the driving seat. He headed back to the road separating Raquel from Yamani. He wasn't too happy about his decision to give the Uzi to Raquel. But she was the soldier-policewoman: he was the geologist.

As he ran, keeping low, he thought about the possibility of mines. Chinese mines, Russian rockets, French artillery, Belgian rifles, Scandinavian light machine guns, British and American tanks . . . the babel of armaments was hardly an inspiration for the United Nations.

He cut through an unkempt garden and paused on the verandah of a bungalow. Through the glassless window he saw a cot containing a doll with no head. The doll appeared to move. Then he saw why—there was a well-fed rat in the cot with the doll. He raised his pistol to shoot it; but the shot would pinpoint his position. The rat stared at him for a moment, shell explosions finding red lights in its eyes. Then it jumped heavily out of the cot and padded off to the kitchen: a rat in full residence.

He came to the road about a hundred yards away from the burning building. He waited for a lull in the shooting so that he would not be illuminated as he crossed. The Egyptian artillery sent over a salvo: the Israelis replied: Bartlett ran across the road and hurled himself behind a low wall skirting a yard.

At the end of the road he could see the outline of the Coptic Church. He investigated the moonlit yard and exclaimed softly: beside him lay the skeleton of a donkey, its bones picked white and clean by rats.

His heart was beating fast, too fast for a forty-year-old, out-of-condition geologist. He decided to rest.

The jeep skidded to a halt a few yards in front of him. He shrank closer to the wall.

An Irish voice, Guinness-rich and potato-thick, said: "Come on out. We saw you go in there."

An Irish voice in a devastated town on the banks of the Suez Canal. Perhaps he was going crazy. Perhaps the whole succession of events had been a fantasy. An Irishman in Kantara. He grinned stupidly in the moonlight.

The voice from the bogs spoke again. "Come on out of there."

Then Bartlett laughed aloud because he had realised who the Irishman was: he was a member of the United Nations. The combination was irresistible.

The Irishman said: "What the hell are you laughing about, whoever you are?"

Bartlett said: "It doesn't matter. But I can't stand up— I'll get shot."

The jeep backed into the yard and the Irishman said: "Get in now and keep your bloody head down."

Bartlett climbed in. "What are you doing here?" he said.

186

The Irishman who was wearing a blue steel helmet considered the question. Then he nodded at his companion, also in a steel helmet, sitting beside him. "Ask him," he said. "He got us out here. Personally I think he's crazy."

"Not so crazy," Ralston said. He turned round. "Hi there, Mr Bartlett. Don't we meet in the darnedest spots?"

Bartlett said: "All right, Ralston, what are you doing here?" He held up the pistol so that Ralston could see it.

"I'll tell you later," Ralston said. "Right now I don't think it's too healthy around here."

As he spoke a rifle barked near the smouldering house. Raquel opened up with the Uzi on the other side of the road.

The Irishman said: "Sweet Mother of God, what's going on up there?"

Bartlett told them. "And Yamani's got grenades," he said.

Ralston said: "This is too far for him to throw them."

Bartlett said: "Raquel isn't too far for him. In any case I expect he's coming down this way."

The black egg landed in the middle of the road about ten yards away from them. It exploded as they dived behind the wall. The wall bent and straightened itself. The Irishman swore and sat up clutching his arm.

Ralston said: "How many grenades has this bastard got?"

"I don't know," Bartlett said.

"We'll have to get him from behind."

"That's what I was going to do before you turned up."

"You stay here. I'll go round the back."

Bartlett said: "No, I'll go round the back."

Ralston said: "I can use a gun—you can't."

"I'm tired of hearing people say that."

"Come on," Ralston said. "Don't play games you don't understand."

Bartlett jammed the pistol in Ralston's ribs. "You stay here," he said.

"Don't be crazy. This guy Yamani is a trained marksman. He'll kill you and he'll kill the girl."

"You look after the Irishman," Bartlett said. "In any case *you* can't go shooting people in a United Nations helmet. You're supposed to be part of a peace-keeping force."

The Irishman, young with a pugilist's face which made no concessions to peace, was swearing and holding his arm. "The bastard's broken," he said. "I wish to Christ I had a gun."

Bartlett said: "His arm's bleeding pretty badly." In the moonlight the blood oozing on to his hand was black. Bartlett prodded the gun barrel in Ralston's ribs. "Put a tourniquet on him. He'll bleed to death otherwise." He was surprised at the authority in his voice.

Ralston said: "For the last time, let me go. You do the nursing."

"Sorry," Bartlett said.

Up the road Raquel's Uzi sprayed bullets into the smouldering building. There was no reply from Yamani.

Ralston said: "Maybe he's getting low on ammunition."

"Maybe," Bartlett said. "You look after the Irishman." He crept out of the back of the yard as a rocket exploded in front of the Coptic Church flinging metal and debris against its patient walls.

Ralston said: "You're nuts."

"Perhaps," Bartlett said. Fear, exaltation, bravado, perhaps, pulsed inside him. A kind of madness maybe. He could taste blood. He had to stop Yamani from killing Raquel. To hell with everything else.

As Bartlett edged into the shadows beyond the moon-bleached bones of the donkey Ralston said: "Hold it."

Bartlett stopped.

Ralston said: "He's running for his jeep. Let's go."

Bartlett jumped into the jeep as it took off with Ralston at the wheel. Ahead of them Yamani's jeep accelerated towards the Canal.

"The girl," Ralston said. "Why the hell doesn't she shoot?"

Raquel opened up but the bullets only flung up dust behind Yamani's jeep.

Ralston slowed down and shouted to her. "There's a man bleeding to death back there. Go help him."

Yamani's jeep rounded a corner.

Ralston said: "Has he got the map?"

"Yes," Bartlett said. "He's got the map."

"Then we've got to stop the bastard." He rammed his foot on the accelerator.

Bartlett didn't reply. As the black and wrecked outlines of Kantara sped past Bartlett realised that the artillery duel had stopped. It was rearmament time.

Chapter 25

Ralston said: "Take a pot shot. Who knows, you might even hit him."

Bartlett leaned out and aimed the big pistol at Yamani's jeep. The gun kicked viciously in his hand. The jeep sped on.

On either side of them the remnants of the town rested after the bombardment. Dogs and rats foraged, walls creaked uneasily.

Their jeep bundled along the shell-pocked road, taking mounds of rubble as if they were miniature ski jumps. But they didn't gain on Yamani.

Ralston said: "I reckon the son-of-a-bitch is heading for the pick-up point on the Canal. Yosevitz seems to have gotten himself an able lieutenant this time."

Bartlett leaned out and took another shot at Yamani. He missed.

"I can't make out what he's aiming to do," Ralston said. "He's got to stop at the Canal. Then he's ours."

"I'm not so sure," Bartlett said. He grinned, for no particular reason, into the silvered night; the slipstream whipped his hair across his face.

Ralston said: "He's slowing up. Keep your head down."

They were rapidly overhauling Yamani now. A hundred yards, seventy-five, fifty. Bartlett raised the pistol and took careful aim. As he fired their jeep jumped a shellhole and the barrel jerked towards the moon.

Yamani's jeep leaped forward, accelerating with a rasp of gears. Bartlett saw the grenade first. He shouted to Ralston and pointed.

Ralston swung the jeep off the road. The explosion of the grenade hurt Bartlett's eardrums. The jeep rocked, almost overturned, then sank back on its wheels.

"The bastard," Ralston said. "How many goddamn grenades has he got?" He swung the jeep back on to the road. "Are you okay?"

"Yes," Bartlett said. "I'm okay."

"Yamani knows he's got to shake us off to stand any chance of getting across the canal," Ralston said. "They'll probably start another bombardment at a fixed time to distract attention from him."

The fleeing jeep rocked round a corner and disappeared.

Ralston said: "I wonder if there's another grenade waiting round the corner for us."

"I wonder," Bartlett said.

"We'll just have to chance it."

Bartlett nodded with the fatalism that had become part of his existence.

They rounded the corner. But there was no grenade waiting for them. And no jeep either.

"Where the hell's he gone?" Ralston said.

The tranquility of the light from the moon and the thick stars seemed to intensify. A dog chased a rat down the road —or it may have been the other way round. The wall of a wrecked house swung gently outwards and fell to the ground. The rest of the house followed thankfully.

Ahead Bartlett saw a line of stumps that had once been buildings, then a gap. The bank of the Canal. The moonlight found a railroad line and coated it with bright ice; a tangle of wires hung from a fractured telegraph pole. The smell in the air had changed subtly: the smell of de Lesseps' dream stagnating.

The devastated buildings and the telegraph pole reminded Bartlett of photographs of the battlefields of the First World

War. The Canal—a water-filled trench dividing Arab and Jew.

Ralston said: "Yamani's around here somewhere. He probably hoped we'd drive past."

"Perhaps he's going on by foot."

"He could be. But he must be going left because the United Nations and the Israeli HQ are to the right."

The engine of Yamani's jeep started up about fifty yards away. The jeep jumped away, skidded off the road and headed across wasteland.

Ralston said: "The UN told me that was laid with mines. The stupid bastard will blow himself up."

"There's no point in chasing him then."

Ralston jumped out of the jeep and shouted after Yamani. "You're in a minefield. Stop where you are. We won't shoot."

The jeep bounced on. They waited in the moonlight smelling the rotting water of the Canal, listening to the creak of the resting buildings.

Bartlett said: "He's halfway across."

"He can't get much farther."

"Who laid the mines?"

"Egyptian commandos maybe. Israelis. Who the hell knows around here."

Yamani was three-quarters of the way across.

Ralston shouted again. "Stop, Yamani. It's suicide." His voice was muffled by the deadness around them.

The first explosion came as Yamani's jeep partially disappeared in a crater. But it wasn't a mine: the Egyptian bombardment had started again.

Ralston said: "It's his cover. They'll have one of those motorboats with French electric engines waiting for him. We'll have to risk following him." He climbed back into the jeep.

Bartlett said: "He's got a long way to go yet."

"Sorry," Ralston said. "We've got to go. At least I've got to go."

"Don't be a fool," Bartlett said.

"I'm going after him."

Yamani's jeep reared up on the other side of the crater. The Egyptian guns were firing continuously but the shells were falling a long way behind Kantara. Then the Israeli guns opened up in reply.

Ralston put the jeep into gear.

Bartlett said: "Let him go. You've won anyway. The map he's got is quite worthless."

Chapter 26

Kantara lay stunned in the dawn light. There were fresh wounds in the desert-coloured buildings along the waterfront. But they no longer had any significance: they were wounds in a corpse.

The pink morsels of cloud in the sky faded and for a while the light was milky fresh. A saline breeze drifted in from the sea moving the surface of the idle water separating sleeping snipers and gunners.

But soon the latent heat, the stagnation and the inevitability of the next bout of shelling asserted themselves. The breeze wandered on towards the Bitter Lakes. The air acquired an oily texture, the ripples on the Canal spent themselves. Doom settled like poisoned gas.

Bartlett, Ralston, and Raquel sat in a dusty room, cushioned outside by sandbags, in the United Nations observation post on the waterfront. A large blue and white UN flag hung outside; the tower on one side of the building had been holed precisely by a shell; the wall on the other side was pitted with small craters like Gruyère cheese.

Behind the UN post the Israelis had dug into bunkers reinforced with railroad tracks.

The UN post was currently occupied by three Irishmen, a Mexican, a Finn, and an Italian.

An Irishman handed Bartlett a mug of coffee and said: "We get it every bloody time. The Gyppos reckon it's because the Israelis always put a tank next door to us." He handed a mug to Raquel. "How's my mate by the way?"

"He'll be all right," Raquel said. "He's been treated at a field hospital. Then he'll be taken to hospital in Tel Aviv."

"What was it all about anyway?" the Irishman said.

Bartlett looked at Ralston and Raquel. "It's a long story," he said. He still hadn't told Raquel the truth: he was sorry in a way that he had been forced to tell Ralston: it was high time they both experienced a little bewilderment.

The Irishman nodded and pushed his blue baseball cap with its white badge on to the back of his head. He wore a blue silk scarf knotted at the neck of his shirt; the words Field Service were printed on his shirtsleeve. "It doesn't matter," he said. "It's always the bloody same. Everyone shooting at us when all we're supposed to be doing is stop the bastards from shooting each other."

Raquel declined the challenge. If it had been tea, Bartlett thought, she would have read *defeat* in the leaves. He immediately felt sorry for her. The Irishman looked disappointed.

Nearby someone fired a rifle.

Ralston said: "Them or us?"

"Them," the Irishman said. "If you mean the Gyppos. A sniper with a Semyonov rifle. Stick your bloody head up around here and they knock it off for you." He stubbed his cigarette in an ashtray made from a shellcase. "Last night a shell fell on top of the billet where we're staying."

No one spoke.

"Well, I'd best be off," the Irishman said. "You'll be leaving here soon?"

They nodded.

"Lucky bastards," he said. "But I'm thinking that you'll be having some explaining to do first."

Ralston said: "I'm thinking there's some explaining to be done around here."

Raquel sat on the edge of a camp bed smoking and sipping her coffee without enthusiasm. Her face was tired and dirty, her hand cut and blistered from the shell splinter. Bartlett regretted his own perversity; but she shouldn't have tried to hand him over to Israeli troops. He sat beside her. "There's something you should know," he said. He put his arm round her.

She examined the smoke from her cigarette. "It doesn't matter. I failed. You were very brave, Thomas. But Yamani's got the map. That's all that matters. That's all I wanted, that's all Ralston wanted." She looked at Ralston and frowned. "Although he does not seem to be very worried."

Ralston shrugged theatrically.

Bartlett sighed. "It was like this," he said. "After the First World War various surveys were carried out. The German did have the task of finding out whether there was any possibility of drilling for oil in certain areas. And I did find his bones—and his maps. One map in particular. But the fact of the matter is that his findings with regard to oil were negative."

Raquel regarded him with disbelief. "Negative?"

"Yes, negative. There is no oil in the areas that he prospected. He had his own system of annotating maps. Every cross on that map means there was no oil." He paused. "I knew about the system. It never occurred to me that anyone would think the crosses meant anything else."

Raquel appealed to Ralston. "Is this true?"

"That's what the guy says."

A sniper fired again across the Canal and the bullet ricocheted past the window.

Bartlett said: "It's all quite logical when you think about it. Apart from the banks of the Gulf of Suez no one's done much about the Sinai since the First World War and it didn't seem likely that anyone was going to do anything about it. Not when I found that map anyway. The map was just a leaf of negative history as far as I was concerned. One or two people know about it. Geologists and ordnance surveyors and suchlike. But no one was really bothered. Least of all me. Although I did think it would be of interest over

196

here. Just interest—nothing more. Because as far as I was concerned it merely showed where there wasn't any oil. Anyway you know what happened . . ."

"You told your wife," she said.

"Correct. A chance remark about maps and oil. I suppose she wanted to impress her Arab boyfriend." He smiled cautiously at Ralston. "And the Americans, of course. Anyway she got it all wrong."

Raquel rounded on him. "Then why did you let me make a fool of myself?" Her face was animated with anger.

"I didn't," Bartlett said. "For most of the time I haven't known what you were all after. Why should I? The maps were of no value as far as I was concerned. Then I realised it must be the maps you wanted. But I still couldn't work out why. By this time an element of perversity had entered the whole thing. Ralston tried to get my briefcase from the Dan Hotel by trickery, an Arab stole it, Yosevitz tried to kill me and you, Raquel, didn't play it straight with me. Not even . . ."

"Not even what?"

"It doesn't matter." He had been going to say, "Not even when you were pretending you loved me."

Raquel said: "I still don't understand." She was sitting cross-legged at one end of the bed, her face puzzled and angry. "Why did you continue this play-acting when you knew it was oil we were after and you also knew the map was worthless?"

"Three reasons," Bartlett said. He was enjoying his role; but it was, after all, his turn. "One—I wanted to see it through. Two—I wanted to be on the winning side."

Raquel frowned. "What was the point of being on the winning side if the maps were of no use anyway?"

"That," Bartlett said, "is where the third reason comes in."

The door opened and the Irishman came in with a jug of fresh coffee which looked like a tankard of stout in his meaty hand. "One dead and one injured last night," he said.

197

Raquel said: "Israelis?"

He nodded.

Her eyes moistened.

The Irishman poured coffee and went out shaking his head.

Raquel said: "What is this third reason?"

Bartlett said: "If you think about it you'll discover that you *have* won. You and Ralston. The whole object of the exercise was to know what areas of the Sinai should be kept and what should be handed over in any negotiations at any level. Right?"

"Right," Ralston said.

"And the Russians and the Arabs now think that they've got the key to the oil potential of parts of the Sinai. Right?"

"Right," Raquel said.

"Then it rather looks to me," Bartlett said, "as if both Israel and the United States are in a pretty handy bargaining position."

Ralston grinned. "You've certainly had me fooled," he said. "In fact we're probably in a better bargaining position than we would have been if we knew where the oil *was*. We can still make the play. When the Soviets and the Arabs find that we're offering to give up territory in which they think there's oil they'll jump at it. And we'll have the—the prestige —of making the offer."

Bartlett said: "Who's *we?*"

Ralston looked speculatively at Raquel. "The Americans or the Israelis. Both perhaps. I'm sure that can be hammered out."

"And now," Bartlett said, "I'd like to get on with what I came here to do. If we can make it, I'd like to get back to Tel Aviv to deliver my paper this afternoon."

Ralston said: "I guess we can make it all right. But there's just one thing."

"What's that?" Bartlett said.

"Could you please forget all about the oil potential of the Sinai when you give this lecture?"

"It will be a pleasure," Bartlett said.

Raquel said: "Thank you, Thomas." She scowled at him and smiled at him at the same time.

So it was all over, Bartlett thought. Back to geology.

Ralston drove. Raquel sat beside him with Bartlett in the back of the jeep. The day was expanding with heat. It seemed to Bartlett that you could smell desert sunshine just as you could smell coffee or Gauloise. The sky was glazed with heat and the sea was jostling with shoals of sunlight.

Bartlett said: "Right, I've answered your questions. How about you answering some?"

Raquel glanced round.

Bartlett said: "No, you Ralston. How did you get to Kantara?"

Ralston said: "You forget that I'm supposed to be a journalist. I came with the other newspapermen covering the exchange of Arabs across the Canal. And then—well, I just stayed."

Raquel looked at him suspiciously. "And the United Nations liked you so much they took you on a night tour of the town?"

"Not quite," Ralston said. "Before I left Jerusalem I got one of our guys who shall be nameless to get in touch with the UN at Kantara. It was pretty obvious that Yosevitz would contact the Arabs and tell them to pick you up at Kantara. So we told the UN that our radio monitors had reason to believe that Arab commandos were operating from a base somewhere on the outskirts of Kantara. The rest was easy. The UN boys got a fix on the radio that Yamani was operating to get his instructions. Then I dropped in on the United Nations after the party of journalists had disappeared and identified myself as the American communication guy responsible for monitoring the Arab radio."

"But you're not," Raquel said.

"No," Ralston said, "I'm not."

Bartlett said: "So you and one Irishman came along in a jeep to clear up a nest of Egyptian commandos?"

"Not quite," Ralston said. "My only reason for being in Kantara was to get that map. So I suggested a reconnaissance tour in the area where they got the fix to get the lay of the land. The UN only sent one guy along because they knew the commandos wouldn't give themselves away by opening up on a UN jeep."

"Why didn't you come by yourself?" Bartlett said.

"Because they wouldn't let me." He waved at a couple of Arab children standing on the roadside. "It's a pity about the Irishman. But he'll live. I reckon you can get export Guinness in Tel Aviv."

A couple of Bedouins and a line of camels materialised between two sand dunes. The sun grew hotter, the long waves tasted the hot beach with apathetic interest.

Bartlett looked at his watch. They would just about make it back to Jerusalem in time for his address.

Then the torpor of the desert overcame him and he half-slept, head-jerking and mouth open, as the jeep sped towards the Eternal City. Such was his fatigue that he hardly heard the big guns as they opened up once again across the water-filled trench called the Suez Canal.

Chapter 27

Ralston attended Bartlett's lecture. He sat at the back of the hall trying to control his yawning boredom. Many members of the audience—some still pale from the explosive aftermath of their Arab meal—seemed equally bored. But perhaps that was how geologists reacted on their own entertainments.

He wasn't quite sure why he had come. Perhaps to see how this deceptively absent-minded Englishman performed, in his own field. He noticed Raquel Rabinovitz sitting two rows in front of him.

After five minutes of rocks, igneous and otherwise, Ralston's thoughts drifted back to his own profession. His colleagues and his adversaries. One adversary at least had left the current scene. Ralston had checked with the hotel and El Al: Yosevitz had caught the London via Munich plane presumably believing that his assignment had been carried out successfully. Ralston's instinct told him that the Israelis might not leave it there: if they killed Yosevitz in London it would look like another Arab outrage . . .

As Ralston considered his own ironic success some of the diamond sparkle returned to his sense of purpose, its lustre enhanced by the thought of Arabs and Russian agents in Cairo exalting over the negotiating material they had captured. He chuckled and a geologist with a face as stony as his work glared at him.

In the end American prestige had been well served. So

201

had the cause of peace in the Middle East. The two were not really incompatible. The diamond positively glittered. Just the same Ralston hoped that on the next mission the considerations would be simpler: them versus us.

By the time Bartlett was two strata under the surface of the Sinai, Ralston decided that enough was enough. He would go back to the hotel and mentally begin his report. Just as he used to at the precinct.

He stood up, apologised to the geologists on either side of him, and left the hall.

As he walked out an American geologist whispered to his neighbour. "You know something," he said, "that guy looks just like a cop."

His neighbour who was an Englishman turned round, stared at Ralston and shook his head. "No," he said, "he looks too much like a policeman to be a policeman."

Chapter 28

They made love that evening in Bartlett's hotel room above Jerusalem. With an ardour and understanding that they had never before experienced.

Then they slept. Two hours later Raquel awoke him. He turned to her and saw in her face that the other questions had to be answered now. He tried to divert them. "What did you think of my address?" he said.

"Very competent," she said. "You are a very clever man, Thomas." She lit a cigarette. "When are you leaving?"

Bartlett had not yet answered this and the other questions to himself. "I haven't made up my mind," he said.

"Yes you have," she said. "Even if you haven't admitted it to yourself." She stroked his face. "Don't lie to yourself or to me, Thomas."

"I suppose I'll leave after the conference," he said. "In two days' time."

"Ah."

He put his hand on her breast but she pushed it away. He waited for the other questions.

She said: "Will you go back to your wife?"

At least he had answered *this* question to himself. "No," he said. "I couldn't do that."

"What will you do then?"

"I don't know yet. You must make allowances for me— I was very set in my ways when I met you."

203

She smiled sadly. "But not any longer, my Thomas."

"Not any longer," he said. "Shall we have a drink?"

"A last drink already?"

"I didn't say that. I've got another two days yet."

"All right," she said. "So we will have a drink. A whisky for me. A large one."

He ordered the drinks and took them from the waiter at the door.

She sipped her whisky, grimaced and took a longer drink. "I have been thinking," she said.

Bartlett took a gulp of his drink to prepare himself for her thoughts. "Yes?" he said.

"Now that the Arabs have the map showing all the places where there isn't any oil it is the duty of us Israelis to find the places where there is oil."

He nodded. "You're already trying to do that."

She ignored him. "And I think it would be very wonderful if you, with all your knowledge of the Sinai, helped them."

He raised himself on one elbow and gazed at the stars shining down on Jerusalem. On the Dome of the Rock, on the Church of the Holy Sepulchre, on the Western Wall. On Arab and Jew and Christian.

"I'll tell you what I'll do," he said. "When I go back to London I'll go straight to Somerset House."

"What is this Somerset House?"

"It's the place where you can trace your ancestors."

"What are you talking about? Surely you are not making fun of me."

"No, I'm not making fun of you. I just want to find out if I've got any Jewish blood in me."

"It would be wonderful if you did," she said. "And then I shall be able to help you in your work in the desert."

"Aren't you rather presuming that I will find I've got some Jewish blood?"

She smiled, lips against his. "Everyone can find Jewish blood in them if they look hard enough."

"Just one other thing," he said.

"And what is that?" Her voice was a murmur.

"How can an expert on water irrigation help a geologist looking for oil. I've always been told that oil and water don't mix."

She pulled him down and showed him.

A few seconds later the phone rang. They stopped and Raquel picked up the receiver.

"Who is it?" he said.

"I don't know," she said. "It's a man. An American, I think."

"It's probably the President of the United States," Bartlett said. "Hang up."